CW00498409

New Fiction

WRITING
CHALLENGE SERIES:
ACROSS A CROWDED ROOM

Edited by

Chiara Cervasio

First published in Great Britain in 2004 by
NEW FICTION
Remus House,
Coltsfoot Drive,
Peterborough, PE2 9JX
Telephone (01733) 898101
Fax (01733) 313524

SB ISBN 1 85929 099 X

FOREWORD

When 'New Fiction' ceased publishing there was much wailing and gnashing of teeth, the showcase for the short story had offered an opportunity for practitioners of the craft to demonstrate their talent.

Phoenix-like from the ashes, 'New Fiction' has risen with the sole purpose of bringing forth new and exciting short stories from new and exciting writers.

Across A Crowded Room is the latest offering from the New Fiction Writing Challenge Series, in which each author has produced a unique and individual piece from an enticing opening set paragraph. Each story goes on to offer an interesting and memorable read that will draw you in to linger broodingly at the back of your mind.

Read on and enjoy the pleasure of that most perfect form of literature, the short story.

Writing Challenge Winner:

Rebecca Nichol - 'The Best Days Of Your Life'

Book Title: A Party Of Strangers

Highly Commended:

Pamela Robson - 'Murder, No Mystery'

Book Title: Across A Crowded Room

S Mullinger - 'Transformation'

Book Title: Across A Crowded Room

CONTENTS

SALES PARTY
Carol C Olson

She sat perched on a chair in her glittery black dress with her perfect curls falling elegantly onto her shoulders. A whole party bustled around her. Hidden in the corner she gracefully sipped her wine, scanning the room for a familiar face. Why has she really bothered coming anyway? A whole bunch of pretentious strangers, slapping each other on the back, congratulating one another on pure hearsay. It had seemed such an excellent idea to try something new, but now it seemed so incredibly wrong. Honestly, what had possessed her to attend a sales party.

Her husband had just made million dollar sales person of the year. She was so very proud of him. He was successful, he believed, due to his beautiful and charming wife.

She had not attended one of these events before. Usually, she was so tired and worn out from the care of the couple's two-year-old twins, that other times she would graciously bow out and go to bed early with the twins.

As she watched from a distance, her beloved telling stories and communicating with others, tonight she was glad she had come. Especially when she observed the red-headed beauty that had sidled up to him, and put her arm on his neck. She immediately rose from the chair, and went over to introduce herself to the redhead.

She had a strong feeling that she would be attending more of these events in the future . . .

THE SHOW IS OVER
Norman Meadows

She sat perched on a chair in her glittery black dress with her perfect curls falling elegantly onto her shoulders. A whole party bustled around her. Hidden in the corner she gracefully sipped her wine, scanning the room for a familiar face. Why has she really bothered coming anyway? A whole bunch of pretentious strangers, slapping each other on the back, congratulating one another on pure hearsay. It had seemed such an excellent idea to try something new, but now it seemed so incredibly wrong. Honestly, what had possessed her to attend a . . .

really up-market celebration for Malcolm, winner of the men's three day event at the International Horse Trials, knowing she would be totally out of her depth? But nonetheless irresistibly drawn by the mysterious invitation arriving in her email the day before!

A circle of admirers hid the victor from her view. She recognised stars of stage and screen, a duo of well-known super-models and a TV chat show host.

But she remained seated, looking beautiful and serene, though feeling insecure and inadequate. She knew the winner well but could not bring herself to approach him, after all, she was only employed by him as a mere stable-hand and groom to his champion horse, Bruno. An out-of-place minion desperately seeking one really familiar face - perhaps the source of her unexpected invite. Or hopefully even someone at her own lowly level. Yet more negative thoughts heightened her discomposure, 'Oh dear, I feel totally outclassed among the glitterati here, I think I'd better split before it gets any worse. Go home, watch telly, have a stiff drink or two. Fall asleep watching telly.'

Failing to make contact she tossed her head dismissively. Long, glossy black curls swirled around, settling to frame her oval features like an exquisite cameo. In this precious but fleeting moment she looked up, preparing to leave. Then she noticed Malcolm had detached himself from the group of admiring sycophants and was walking towards her, staring intently!

'Here comes the courtesy call,' she mused. 'Two minutes flat, heigh-ho, away we go. The show is over!'

To her surprise he greeted her warmly. 'Hi Kate - so you got my email. Terribly pleased you could make it. Can I get you a refill?'

Kate suddenly felt as if she had taken one too many already; here he was, the man of the moment, actually paying her attention! She stammered a reply and watched as he body-swerved his way through the crowd. Accosted by women and men alike it was some time before he got back, arriving with an almost half-empty glass.

'Sorry dear - it's worse than a point-to-point out there!'

'Oh, I thought you'd been waylaid by one of the model girls,' she replied letting her insecurities show.

'No, indeed no! A coat hanger has little room for brains.'

A bit chauvinistic, she thought but let it pass. As they chatted together what she had at first thought was an insurmountable gap in their ages now seemed insignificant. Their conversation flowed easily; he even touched her hand occasionally, sending electric shocks from her fingers down to her toes!

The past six weeks had been wonderful: pictures of them on the front pages of the tabloids, rumours of an impending marriage. Kate was still highly excited following their whirlwind drive to Vienna to see the Lippizaner dressage show, seated in the best grandstand seats with Malcolm competing on other top-class horses, back via Cannes and its casinos, then on to Paris and London.

It had not been easy to maintain her strong belief that sex before marriage was not for her. Heavy petting, yes, but she would not go all the way - at least, not yet. Malcolm seemed to be unfazed and Kate was grateful for his self-control. Their relationship blossomed, perhaps, she thought from time to time, rather because of, than in spite of, her reserved position.

In the coming months she dedicated herself to Malcolm and Bruno, working long hours to help them reach their peak for the forthcoming championships. Kate was happier than she had ever been, loving the stable smells, dark polished leather, musty hay, the silky sweat from the horses after exercising. Even the many different aromas given off by feeds and embrocations, the delicious sensation of Bruno caressing her with his warm breath while nuzzling her outstretched palm for half an apple. And, above all, she loved the sweet smell of success!

Returning home late one evening she scanned her email: among genuine messages and loads of spam, one item caught her eye. It was an invitation from a media company undertaking to attempt to find lost friends and relatives, mentioning in particular, a change in the law, whereby adopted children were now free to try to trace their natural parents. Kate had long hoped she might one day accomplish this, so she replied with the necessary details and waited.

There was little she and Malcolm did not share, but Kate saw this as a singular event and anyhow it might well come to nothing. So life continued happily, although arduously and happenings around her dominated her thoughts. Until one day a letter arrived . . .

The producers of the show 'Dare You Face Your Past?' invite you for a preliminary discussion at their London studios . . .

Kate fibbed, 'I've been invited to a chat show where celebrities' partners are asked to speak about their lives . . .' The truth could be revealed later - if necessary.

The researchers were very competent: within a month they had tracked down her natural parents, discovering that Kate's mother had married an oil executive who spent most of his time overseas. During one of these absences she met another man, conceiving a child by him. Fortunately for her, the consequences did not show too evidently and, even more fortunately, her husband was away for the last three months and beyond full term. But unfortunately for her, also around the time of conception.

She decided to have the baby adopted quickly before her husband returned, raiding a joint bank account to facilitate a quick, but illegal, adoption. The researchers were told she explained the large debit away as a cash payment for the new car in the drive. With her HP agreement tucked safely away in a gap at the back of her dressing-table drawer.

But her husband found out! After the divorce she turned back to her daughter's natural father and they married. Wishing to set the past behind her, she and her new partner emigrated to Australia, while her son by the previous marriage stayed back in England

Because of the illegality of the so-called adoption, the producers had wisely chosen not to put Kate's adoptive parents in the frame. But they had uncovered more skeletons in the cupboard - which they deliberately kept locked away, intending to spring surprises on the participants to enhance the show's dramatic effect. Kate was kept mostly in the dark, given only a few bits of information. An ambush was being set!

Then a letter arrived asking if she would be prepared to meet her natural parents. She read it with mixed feelings, nervous and apprehensive. Nonetheless she agreed.

Knowing she must soon tell Malcolm, Kate rang her best friend and confidant Angela, recounting the main details and adding, 'But I'm still not sure of the outcome - it may be premature.'

'Would you like a shoulder to cry on if it all goes pear-shaped?'

'That's nice of you Angela, but I think I'll tough it out on my own. Thanks a lot just the same dear.'

'Well catch up with me later and meantime remember my offer. Cheers. See you at the championships.'

Eventually Kate decided to keep her own counsel - at least for the time being.

The great moment had arrived: the third day of the championships and with it the finals. The grandstand crowd buzzed with excitement. Kate gripped her programme tightly. Competition was world-class standard, fiercely determined and seemingly unstoppable. Only one point - a time fault - now separated the last two riders. After three days of intense competition.

'Here comes Malcolm Degros on Bruno. He needs a clear round to win.' The pseudo-classy voice brayed out over the distorting PA system, against a background of muted aircraft noise, coming from the direction of a distant airfield where a worldwide air show was being hosted.

Kate turned to her friend, 'That's not too clever, Angela. I wonder why they coincide the events?'

'Weather conditions apparently. There's been trouble before but now the organisers have guaranteed that there will be no over-flying, so it will be OK.'

'I hope so, Malcolm will need every ounce of concentration if he's to win against this level of competition.'

'Sure will,' Angela replied laconically.

Malcolm cantered Bruno into the show ring, to the resonance of the 'one time fault' following his predecessor's exit from the arena. Mounting applause greeted the home rider's clearances - the double, triple, water jump . . . Malcolm put Bruno into a tight turn, head down he charged at the last and highest fence.

At that moment a fighter jet with Chinese insignia streaked across the arena, breaking the sound barrier. But not the language barrier it seemed! A sonic boom thundered. Spooked unbearably, Bruno dug in his front hooves and skidded to a stop. Malcolm did not. Bruno swerved right, Malcolm swerved left, one foot trapped in his stirrup. Kate screamed as an ominous double crack accompanied his undignified fall onto the churned-up turf.

She accompanied the helicopter to the nearby hospital. The A & E staff hurried Malcolm into a waiting area, called for the orthopaedic surgeon on duty, acquainted him with the problem and who was involved. The severity of the compound fractures to Malcolm's leg warranted quick attention. He was prioritised on the triage, X-rays and pre-diagnosis case notes were hurried to the operating theatre. Soon the surgeon was bent over Malcolm beneath the theatre lights, already anticipating the spotlights that would illuminate him; interviews for television, the morning papers . . .

Just before the anaesthetic took effect, Malcolm gasped, 'How's Bruno?'

Two traumatic episodes in one day were almost too much for Kate. It was now late evening and the area around the clock at Victoria Station was buzzing.

'I'll never find them in this crowd, red carnations or not. I expect there'll be dozens of people waiting to be button-holed.' She smiled wryly to herself at her innocent quip, but it was a fleeting smile. In a state of near panic she edged closer to the group of people around the clock base. Waiting. Wondering. Hoping. Rehearsing words she half-way knew she would never speak under the stress of the occasion. Her mouth was dry, palms sweaty, fingers trembling.

Kate was puzzled, a middle-aged woman stood out, wearing a red carnation, holding a card. Recognising Kate's distinctive blue hat she beckoned to her. As Kate approached nervously, the woman queried, 'Are you Kathryn dear?'

'Er, yes, and you are . . . ?'

'Well the program director tells me . . . er, it seems I'm your mother.'

'Oh, and where's my dad?'

'He's stuck at the airport in Sydney - some security scare or another. I came on ahead of him, so here I am! I'm afraid there's worse to come Kathryn - my son - I suppose he would be your half-brother wouldn't he - has had an accident, thrown from his horse and I must go on to the hospital to see him. I'm so sorry. Perhaps though you'd like to come with me - maybe it's not the best venue, but at least it's something. You may have heard of him - he's quite famous you know.'

'Was that Bruno?' Kate queried.

The woman frowned, 'No - er - his name's Malcolm, that's his . . .'

Kate interrupted urgently, 'The horse I mean! Was it Bruno?'

'Yes, of course. But why did you say that?'

'Is he alright?'

'No dear, I'm afraid Bruno won't ever jump again.'

Kate turned away, fleeing erratically through the crowded concourse. She was not to know the show organisers had been expecting something like this - their show came first, personal feelings a poor second. But the deceit had backfired!

As she tried, but failed, to out-sprint the television cameraman, filming her panicky exit an earworm tunnelled savagely into her brain, 'The show is over . . . the show is over . . . the show is over!'

THE INTERVENTION OF FATE
Mai Edden

She sat perched on a chair in her glittery black dress with her perfect curls falling elegantly onto her shoulders. A whole party bustled around her. Hidden in the corner she gracefully sipped her wine, scanning the room for a familiar face. Why has she really bothered coming anyway? A whole bunch of pretentious strangers, slapping each other on the back, congratulating one another on pure hearsay. It had seemed such an excellent idea to try something new, but now it seemed so incredibly wrong. Honestly, what had possessed her to attend an . . .

end of the course party. She had enjoyed the class, she was surprised when the results had been issued as this class had been difficult to reach, debate hadn't existed. So when they all passed their final exam with flying colours she breathed a sigh of relief. It had been a mixed group of all ages with an eager need to master the art of creative writing.

Some already had degrees in English language and literature, but somehow felt their education wasn't complete until they had written and published a book of their own. Ideas passed around enthusiastically but with this class, fifty percent adult students, she had felt they had put a distance between her and them and sometimes felt the class tutorials could have easily governed themselves. So why was she here, dressed up to the nines, in her one and only glittery black dress, they were strangers to her.

It was because one particular student had arisen in her a curious desire to delve into their background. Geoff wasn't particularly handsome, although being thirty, the early signs of maturity were creeping up and greying hair speckled his sideburns. She thought it was his shyness bordering on being a greater listener than communicator that attracted her, it seemed to create an air of mystery around him, more usual in women than men.

He smiled that half smile she had missed when tutorials were over, she couldn't even discuss his coursework with him she felt so uncomfortable. Tonight she must say hello and talk about their lives at home, after all she was like them now, just a single woman looking for a like-minded friend.

Her past life hadn't been easy, her only son Jake was born when she was a teenager and had been brought up by his father Tim and his parents. University life had no room for the routine a new baby needed, so she made the choice that he was better off in a family environment with Tim's parents, who were only too eager to care for their grandchild. There was no question of marriage to Tim, she didn't love him and consequently, Tim joined his parents when they emigrated to Canada and settled there. This situation eventually led to her relationship breaking down and therefore so did any communication with Jake. Life as a student was easy for her, her passion for literature of all kinds was her first love, so she neatly filed away any thoughts of Tim and Jake, convincing herself it was all for the best.

Susie the youngest of the group had sensed her awkwardness and came over, 'Come and join us, come and meet my fiancée Geoff. You know him of course. We are getting married in two weeks. It's local and we would love you to come to the church, it's at St Stephen's, near the University, 3 o'clock on Saturday afternoon,' she said.

She sat stunned, whatever was she thinking of, she a woman in her late forties mooning over a young man like that. She had an enjoyable evening after that, having resigned herself to being a mature person who unfortunately, had allowed her youth to pass her by.

She arrived at the church at 2.45pm in her new two-piece suit and chose a pew at the back, on the bride's side of the aisle. Geoff, with his back to her, was in the front row on the other side and after enquiring, apparently by his side was his father, who had never married.

Susie arrived radiantly dressed in pink, due to her unconventional nature. The service went on for another twenty minutes and they then all filed out. You can imagine her surprise, when Geoff's father suddenly walked up behind her, she turned round and to her horror, she came face to face with Tim, Jake's father. All she could think of was how handsome he still was and there was that little half smile, that had entered her life when Geoff had joined her evening class. Of course Tim's father's name was Geoff, I expect he must be deceased now and Jake had taken his name.

He didn't recognise her and she didn't pursue the matter but somehow found consolation in the fact that she had attended her son's wedding and regained a relationship of sorts with him. She had peace of mind knowing that Susie had kept up her friendship and that she had become godmother to her godson Jake, gratefully accepting that their paths were meant to cross in such a fateful way.

A LOVE MEETING
J Bradbury

She sat perched on a chair in her glittery black dress with her perfect curls falling elegantly onto her shoulders. A whole party bustled around her. Hidden in the corner she gracefully sipped her wine, scanning the room for a familiar face. Why has she really bothered coming anyway? A whole bunch of pretentious strangers, slapping each other on the back, congratulating one another on pure hearsay. It had seemed such an excellent idea to try something new, but now it seemed so incredibly wrong. Honestly, what had possessed her to attend a . . . dance.

She had rushed from the office to get her hair set into a nice style. Dreaming of a prince charming coming over to ask her to dance, everyone seemed so happy with their escorts.

Was it wise for me to accept the invitation to come to this New Year's Eve ball she thought. All the county toffs were there and she felt no one wanted to meet her.

Suddenly a handsome young man came into the hall. Tall with dark hair looking like an Adonis. He was the son of a rich local farmer. He looked around the crowded room. Their eyes met and he gave her the most beautiful smile. Suddenly he strolled across the floor and asked her to dance.

After the first dance he asked her name and if she was a local girl. He walked her back to her seat and thanked her for the dance.

She did not feel like a wallflower now and hoped he would ask her to dance again. But her hopes began to slip as looking across the floor, she saw him laughing and joking with one of the most beautiful girls she had ever seen. Still as the evening went on, he seemed to have lost interest in this beauty and asked her once again to dance.

They talked and danced for the rest of the evening. The more they danced the more friendly they got. Before the evening was over you would think they were long-lost friends.

She felt the expense of the dress and hair-do was well worth having.

That night ended up in a lifetime of love.

SINGLES PARTY
Kathleen Townsley

She sat perched on a chair in her glittery black dress with her perfect curls falling elegantly onto her shoulders. A whole party bustled around her. Hidden in the corner she gracefully sipped her wine, scanning the room for a familiar face. Why has she really bothered coming anyway? A whole bunch of pretentious strangers, slapping each other on the back, congratulating one another on pure hearsay. It had seemed such an excellent idea to try something new, but now it seemed so incredibly wrong. Honestly, what had possessed her to attend a . . .

singles party, for looking round there was no one here she could even think of fancying and why everyone was congratulating each other she could not even try to understand, after all no one had paired off yet and she had been sat here over one hour. *Oh no,* she thought as everyone's car keys were collected and placed in a huge bowl. *Thank God I came by taxi,* she thought. Pushing herself further into the corner she observed the proceedings and watched as the women giggled when it was their turn to select a key. *How on Earth can they do that? Okay I suppose if you get a David Beckham look-alike, but what happens when you choose the Hulk, what are you supposed to do, smile happily and talk about his lovely shade of green, caused by the fact that you have slapped his face for not controlling his hands?*

How was she to get away from here? Too late, why at this precise time did she get pins and needles in her right foot? Why did she ignore the feeling and remain still, instead of shaking her leg around, giving the men a certain come on.

'Join in love don't be shy,' the men called, 'don't be a party pooper, come and select a key.'

I would rather boil myself in oil, she thought, *than walk into that crowd and pick a key;* then again, she thought, it would give her great satisfaction to push it down the Hulk's throat.

Stepping away from the corner, a huge cheer went up, followed by lecherous grins appearing on some of the older men's faces. *No chance,* she thought, and turning to the left walked straight past the waiting group and collected her coat which had been thrown over the chair. *Thank God they had not put their coats in a huge bowl,* she thought, then marching straight to the door, let herself out, slamming the door behind her.

It had started to pour down and she was feeling shivery and cold by the time she reached the taxi stand, her hair was now plastered around her face, her mascara was running in lines down her cheeks and to top it all she had begun to sneeze her head off. At last a taxi arrived to take her come. Climbing into the cab, she sneezed all the way home, the taxi man scarcely touched her hand when she gave him the money. She knew he thought she had the dreaded flu and he was seriously determined he was not going to catch it. He could not pull away from the kerb fast enough and succeeded in drowning her feet, so not only would she sneeze her way to the flat, but she would squelch all the way as well.

Finally after dripping and squelching up the communal steps of the flats she arrived at her front door. While searching for her door keys amongst wet tissues in her coat pocket, she heard the door opposite her open. Keeping her back towards the opposite door she pulled out her keys amidst a soggy handful of tissues when a voice said, 'Hello, I'm your new neighbour, moved in three days ago. I have been trying to catch you but kept missing you. I am having a flat warming party and wondered if you would like to come.'

Oh no, she thought, *I never want to hear the word 'party' for the rest of my life. All I want to do is have a bath and get into my pyjamas.*

Turning round slowly, she looked at her new neighbour and immediately sneezed into his face. Grabbing the dripping tissues she apologised, then collecting the bits of tissue still attached to her face, said, 'As you can see I am not really prepared for a party. Nice of you to ask but the answer is no.' Then she sneezed once again into the wet tissues. Opening her door, she entered the flat and closed the door quietly behind her, quickly stripping out of her clothes she settled down into a lovely hot bath. When the doorbell rang, she turned the radio up and continued to relax in the bath whilst she listened to classical music. Now sitting in her armchair with a hot cup of tea, wearing her teddy bear pyjamas with panda slippered feet resting nicely on the foot stool, she began to feel a little better.

When the doorbell rang again she plodded to the front door. Pulling the door open, once again she met the eyes of the young man from the opposite flat. 'I see you are feeling better,' he said, 'now will you come to my party?'

She looked at him with amazement. 'Can you tell me,' she said, 'which part of the word no you do not understand.' Looking at his crestfallen face, she apologised immediately for it was not his fault she had gone to the singles party.

As he turned to go, muttering a 'Sorry for disturbing you,' she said, 'Wait, if you are having a party it sounds very quiet.'

He looked at her and said, 'that is probably because no one has turned up. It seems I have picked a night when a singles party has been arranged. Just my luck wouldn't you think. It must be better than mine.'

She had to smile then, then she asked, 'If I come to your party do I have to bring my car keys?'

He looked at her with such a blank expression, she knew he had never been to a singles party.

'OK,' she said, 'but do you mind if we have a pyjama party for I have just got warm and I feel so comfortable now.'

'Not at all,' he said, then taking hold of her hand he said, 'my name's Mark, pleased to meet you.'

'I am Melinda,' she said, then turned to go back into the flat.

She was just finishing drying her hair when the doorbell rang again. *Who on Earth is it now,* she thought and once again made her way to the front door. When she opened her door, standing before her was Mark, wearing puppy dog pyjamas, St Bernard slippers on his feet, holding a bottle of wine and a huge bag of crisps. 'I thought I would bring the party to you, then you can remain all cosy and warm. I hope I am not over dressed.'

She began to smile, then she began to laugh and soon they were both laughing so hard they did not hear or see the neighbour from above leaning over the rail to see what all the noise was about.

'Come in,' she said between fits of the giggles and she closed the door behind him. She went into the kitchen after showing him into the little front room and brought back two glasses. She found him sitting in the opposite arm chair with his slippered St Bernard feet upon the foot stool belonging to that chair. He was about to stand when she said, 'Don't get up, you look settled there.'

'I am,' he said, 'this is such a cosy room, I feel right at home here.' She smiled and passed him a glass, then opening the wine she filled their glasses, sitting down opposite him she too put her feet up on the foot stool and settled back in her armchair.

Silence prevailed for a long time while they both sipped their wine and enjoyed the dancing flames from the fire. 'Why did you ask if you needed your cars keys?' he asked, 'I have not brought mine as I was not sure if that was what one did at a party. Having only just moved to this area from abroad, I am a little confused by your question.'

This set her off giggling again. When she had got her breath back she told him of her evening. He laughed with her and said, 'Now I know why that party was more inviting than mine. They did invite me but I said no and I am glad I did now,' he said, looking at her over the top of his glass.

She felt a flush rise to her cheeks. Changing the subject she asked, 'Do you want to stay for supper, it is not much, just some leftover soup and fresh bread I made earlier.'

'Yes please,' he said, 'need a hand?'

'No thank you I can manage,' and she left him sitting comfortably by the fire whilst she busied herself in the kitchen.

Soon they were sitting at the small dining table by the window eating fresh bread with home-made soup.

'This is lovely, you must give me the recipe.' She looked at him in amazement. 'I love cooking and I know it may seem strange but I enjoy baking too.'

'It is not strange,' she said, 'for I too love being in the kitchen and spend many an evening pouring over recipe books then adapting them to my own use.' Before long they were talking like old friends and the time just flew by.

The man who lived in the flat above was just coming down the stairs at five-thirty in the morning, heading off to work at the local factory. It was his week for the six to two shift, not one of his favourite weeks but it had to be done. When stopping dead at the top of the stairs, was amazed to see two young people chatting in the middle of the corridor in their pyjamas and funny looking slippers. He backed into the shadows not wishing to cause them any embarrassment as well as himself, but after standing there for five minutes, he realised that he could have walked past them stark naked and neither of them would have noticed. He was going to descend the stairs when the man kissed the girl's cheek and went to his own apartment. After the girl closed her own door, he descended the stairs and closed the outside door. As he was driving to work he thought to himself, *the wife is right, it is time to think about moving to the bungalow we have always wanted. I will call at the estate agents this afternoon and look into this. I should have listened to her, she was right these flats are changing, no longer for our age group. There will be all sorts of carrying on before long and I have no intentions of being invited to any of them. I have heard all about them single nights, the sooner we move the better.*

After closing her door she made a cup of coffee, then after opening the curtains, sat in the dining chair by the window, her elbows propped on the table. She watched the neighbour from upstairs drive away. *I would not like to do shift work like him,* she thought and continued to sip her coffee, thinking of the evening's events. There was something about her new neighbour Mark and she wished to get to know him better. She was just thinking how she hoped he was thinking of her at this time when the doorbell rang. Standing up she walked to the door, speaking to the door she called, 'Who's there?'

'Only me,' said Mark, 'thought you might like to try these new breakfast rolls I baked last night, before you accepted my invitation to your pyjama party.'

She thought that over in her head and knew it sounded wrong but she brushed it to one side and opened the door. 'I would love to,' she said and closing the door behind him, went to put the kettle back on to boil.

A SMART LADY
Anne Lewis

She sat perched on a chair in her glittery black dress with her perfect curls falling elegantly onto her shoulders. A whole party bustled around her. Hidden in the corner she gracefully sipped her wine, scanning the room for a familiar face. Why has she really bothered coming anyway? A whole bunch of pretentious strangers, slapping each other on the back, congratulating one another on pure hearsay. It had seemed such an excellent idea to try something new, but now it seemed so incredibly wrong. Honestly, what had possessed her to attend a . . . old school's reunion?

She had never been back in the thirty years but because she was on a list she still received the invitation. So it was in small part curiosity compounded by boredom and having nothing better do that brought her here. This was the whole trouble. She was so, so bored.

Until they moved here life in London never palled. She had a pleasant part-time job in a Kensington hat shop, not large but very smart. The clientele smart, well spoken, not young but not old, their husbands were generally *something in the city,* their children either at college or away - in fact young adults.

Wendy belonged to a local literary club - monthly luncheons with a speaker and with her husband, had joined a bridge club. So life was good. Now here she was at Peter's insistence in this small village with just one shop and five miles from the local market town. Peter had retired early and wanted, what he believed to be an idyllic country life, gardening and joining the local golf club. Quite a good one full of retired, pot-bellied over 60s.

She was proud that she had managed to keep her trim figure, despite two now adult children. So she had made the effort to dress as stunningly as possible, though she was well aware from the sideways glances shot at her that she had gone over the top. However, seeing all these people, some of whom had been at school with her was not cheering. It was a misspent effort. Mostly run to seed, overweight and talked endlessly about their children. So now what on earth was she to do. There was the Women's Institute. She had been taken to a monthly meeting. No heaven forbid. Fraternising with those complacent housewives. Then the last resort. Leave Peter and join John. Tedious as even John could be but with unbelievable Greek god looks, he did at least live on the French Riviera near Monte Carlo enjoying plenty of hot sun, vino, pleasant company and wonderful shopping, though probably because of the prices more often than not shop gazing. He had asked her often enough.

So I suppose leave a note for Peter and adieu here I come.

Peter's wry reaction was, 'I hope the silly woman will be happy,' and relief. She had been impossible to satisfy for practically years. Leaving muddy foot marks on the kitchen floor, calling the dog and whistling happily, he went out feeling carefree, admiring the massed Michaelmas daisies in passing.

THE PARTY
Judith Halford

She sat perched on a chair in her glittery black dress with her perfect curls falling elegantly onto her shoulders. A whole party bustled around her. Hidden in the corner she gracefully sipped her wine, scanning the room for a familiar face. Why has she really bothered coming anyway? A whole bunch of pretentious strangers, slapping each other on the back, congratulating one another on pure hearsay. It had seemed such an excellent idea to try something new, but now it seemed so incredibly wrong. Honestly, what had possessed her to attend a . . . Bagnold and Bagnold Christmas fancy dress party?

After all she had only been with the firm for a week. Any excuse would have done, but no, she had been weak as water as usual.

'Come on Virginia,' they had said, 'don't be a spoil sport! It's the event of the year, everyone's going to be there. It will be the ideal place to meet everyone.'

So here she was. But where were the people who had persuaded her to come? The whole room was full of strangers, loud, effusive, repugnant strangers.

She could hear snatches of conversation all round her. 'Do you remember the year that Sally from accounts came as Nell Gwynn?' she heard one young woman giggle, 'That certainly got her promotion, the boss came as Charles II!'

'They say Mr Bagnold is coming as Julius Caesar this year,' another voice muttered, 'the laurel wreath covers his receding hairline you know.' A few sniggers followed this comment.

Virginia felt faintly sick. She had left her last job to get away from office gossip. What if they should find out about her in this new job and the whispering started all over again? She got up stealthily and began to make her way round the wall to the door. No one noticed her, she was within two yards of it, she made a dash for it - only to collide with someone very solid coming the other way. She drew back, winded and realised that she had hit Maureen the typing pool supervisor.

'Why Virginia,' she cried, 'you do look good, I love the black dress and the wig is just perfect.' She hesitated for a moment. 'Who are you meant to be?'

Virginia thought fast, but no inspiration came. 'I don't really know, she said lamely, I bought this wig years ago and I found an old cocktail dress of my mother's.'

Maureen guffawed with laughter. 'Lucky you to be slim enough to borrow clothes. I always have to come as someone big. To save you asking I am meant to be Boudicea.' She looked closely at Virginia. 'You're not sneaking off are you?' Linking arms firmly she towed the reluctant Virginia back into the room. Come on cheer up, let's go and get our free glass of wine!'

As they passed a group of revellers, Virginia heard a voice whisper, 'Who's she? That dress is terrible.' This was followed by muffled laughter.

'I don't know she must be new.'

Virginia shuddered inwardly, obviously these people loved gossip, what if they discovered about her past? How would she face the embarrassment all over again?

Maureen turned to her, obviously she had heard nothing. 'Now let's see,' she said, 'is there anyone handsome or interesting I can introduce you to? Peter,' she said, 'can I introduce you to Virginia?'

A tall young man turned, dressed as Samuel Pepys, Virginia guessed. 'Why hello,' he said, 'I'll have to mention you in my diary,' he laughed. She smiled politely and waited for the inevitable question but instead he said, 'Marilyn Monroe? It has to be with that perfect figure and that gorgeous blonde hair.'

Virginia found herself speechless.

'We'll have to go Peter,' Maureen said, 'I have just spotted the drinkies tray.'

Virginia drifted on in Maureen's wake. It all seemed like a dream. All decisions were being made for her. She only had to go where she was being led.

She was brought back to Earth by another snatch of conversation.

'Yes, the one in the black dress, they say she was caught in bed with the boss at her last job.'

'Surely not she doesn't look capable of it!'

Virginia's dream crashed into a nightmare. They had discovered already. She felt rising panic. What was she to do? Explain? Nobody would understand if she did. Mr Winters has been so lonely, of course she had been a fool to herself. But then she was weak as everyone knew. If he hadn't told her about his illness and about how his wife was no longer interested . . . she hadn't even loved him really. Of course there had been a terrible row when it all came out and she had been the one who was asked to leave. He hadn't even stood up for her, that was what hurt, he had just let her take the blame. He had telephoned afterwards and tried to explain, she couldn't even be really angry. He was weak too she realised.

She was far away in thought, when she heard her name being called. 'Miss Virginia Lutterworth are you here? Ah yes I see that you are, would you be so kind as to come forward please.'

She felt herself being pushed gently. She walked on in a state of shock still. When she arrived she was helped up the stairs onto the stage and felt her hand being warmly shaken by the company chairman.

'Miss Lutterworth has joined us from Winters Associates as our new investment manager,' he was saying, 'she comes with a very distinguished record and a glowing recommendation from her previous employers. We look forward to her using her expertise to make wise investments for our company's future.'

The faces below her looked up expectantly and a polite round of applause greeted her.

To her surprise, Virginia found herself slipping into her professional persona, she smiled, 'I very much look forward to working with all of you,' she said. As she stepped down from the stage she felt that the atmosphere had subtly changed. People were coming forward to shake her hand and welcome her. Out of the corner of her eye she saw one of the group of gossipers approaching with her hand held out. 'I just love your dress,' she was saying, 'so clever of you to think of it.'

Virginia turned just as the woman arrived, pretending she hadn't noticed her. 'Maureen,' she said, taking her arm as she passed, 'have you found where the drinks are yet?'

'Over here,' Maureen replied cheerfully, 'wonderful snub,' she whispered, 'keep up the good work!'

MARRY ME MARI
Carol Ann Darling

She sat perched on a chair in her glittery black dress with her perfect curls falling elegantly onto her shoulders. A whole party bustled around her. Hidden in the corner she gracefully sipped her wine, scanning the room for a familiar face. Why has she really bothered coming anyway? A whole bunch of pretentious strangers, slapping each other on the back, congratulating one another on pure hearsay. It had seemed such an excellent idea to try something new, but now it seemed so incredibly wrong. Honestly, what had possessed her to attend . . . a Christmas Eve gathering at a public house, the Dead Pan Arms, in the next town to where she lived.

Was it really over with her proposed engagement to Julius? Julius, yes him, named after Julius Caesar. Well, his mother was well into reading about the Roman Empire. *She was just niggled by him*, she thought despairingly. This was the first time she had ever done this sort of thing, venturing out on her own without a friend, or Julius to accompany her. She thought it would be exciting; that some interesting person would just have something intelligent to say that would make this whole Christmas scenario less boring, more bearable, even desirable. *I mean, what is it all about?* she thought, even more despairingly this time. Christmas was always so grey and mundane. She gazed hopefully at the real Christmas tree, decorated so dazzlingly, with silver stars and icicles (a little like my dress, all sparkly). The magic of Christmas was a promise that just didn't seem to materialise, however much she desired that it would. She didn't want to feel so negative or sit like a wallflower. In fact, coming out had been a positive decision, since the break with Julius, hadn't it?

A new start, that was it. She had to face life without Julius. Her mind was a tangle of questions and confusion reigned supreme.

She looked around the busy, noisy room. Do these people here really have happiness? Is this Christmas just a charade to them too? Are they just actors and actresses smiling and going through the motions of what can I buy you to drink old chap, chapess, whatever? How could she be sure of anything anymore? Who would stand by her, give her honour and respect? Who could bring her magic and fun and who could she give all this to too? Not to or from Julius, that was now obvious.

Even these fancy clothes she was wearing were just a mockery. Just a cover of her true feelings. Smart clothes can't change how she feels inside. Of this, she had no doubt.

As the run-off-her-feet barmaid Rita collected up the empty glasses from the tables, she placed a piece of torn paper on Mari's table. 'From the man in the left hand corner there, sitting on his own. Said to give it to you,' mumbled Rita vacantly to Mari, as she continued on to the next table for more empties.

She picked up the scruffy scrap of paper and read to herself, *it's all happening at 7pm Mari, through the main doors.* She glanced surreptitiously over to the corner but nobody was there and she couldn't remember if anyone had been sitting there. *How does anyone know my name? It's a bit of a mystery. Well it doesn't matter,* she thought, putting her hand to her head because she was feeling dizzy.

She decided to go home. She wasn't staying any longer with all the milling pretence. She shouldn't have come. It wasn't for her after all and still holding the shabby note, she gathered up her cutie coat and matching brag bag and headed for the main doors. 'Goodnight everyone,' she mumbled, 'happy Christmas.'

As she opened the doors a force of freezing cold air took her breath and an explosion of white blinded her for a second. She couldn't believe it. She shivered, spellbound as the snowflakes danced before her astonished eyes and softly landed on her lashes and hair. The scintillating scenery was just a splendid surprise.

'Hello, I am a Helf. Have you your ticket?' enquired the perky Helf.

'Ticket, what ticket?' replied Mari smiling.

'There it is,' said the Helf, 'in your hand.'

'Do you mean this piece of paper?'

'That is it,' responded the Helf pleasantly, 'it's the one I sent you. My name is Olav Helf and you are Mari, I know.'

'I don't understand,' said Mari a little nervously, 'it's all so beautiful.'

'We know,' said Olav Helf, 'how much you long for the magical shimmering ice crystal Christmas that we from *The Way To The North* are accustomed to. I mean just look at your glittering dress. You will never find that special beautiful feeling you are searching and long for in there.' Olav Helf pointed to the Dead Pan Arms. 'I know your loving heart. I know your thoughts, your desires and the treasures of your dreams.'

She looked shyly at Olav Helf and little tears were freezing, making ice diamonds on her happy face. The pure, soft snow was falling faster, covering all the trees and land in a white, snug blanket. She hadn't seen snow for years, since she was a child. She wanted to run and throw snowballs just as years ago. Delight was beginning to radiate. Her heart was singing merrily. As she turned to look back at The Dead Pan Arms, it was just an inky blur, a foggy haze, all within there, just a drab memory.

Out in the crisp, cloudy night air, children and adults were skating with colourful hats, gloves and scarves, bobbing as they jumped and raced, or glided serenely to their own dance on the frozen grey pond. Brightly lit market stalls were selling fudge, fruit and mulled wine.

'Now that looks good,' she said to Olav Helf in hungry fashion.

Everywhere people were dressed and muffled up for the ever falling, silky snow from the creamy sky. She danced and swayed in a sort of drunken glee. Gathering snow, she moulded it into a ball and shouted, 'Look out Olav Helf,' as she fell over laughing and Olav Helf took the snowball full force on his head. As she stood up she could hear bells ringing.

'Here is your sled and reindeer Mari,' said Olav Helf.

She climbed in eagerly and they were away, along the mountain pathways, bells dinging, her heart still singing.

'I'm not going back to those former times at The Dead Pan Arms ever,' said Mari and such was her enthusiasm that she kissed Olav Helf on the forehead!

In a striking, brilliant flash, sitting beside her was a tall young man. 'You've broken the spell that a twisted troll put on me, turning me into a Helf,' said Olav Helf excitedly. 'My name is Olav Halvdan. Just call me Olav. Marry me Mari, then you can stay in our snowflake world.' As a promise, he took a snowflake ring from his finger and placed it on a finger of Mari's that it fitted. 'We will be happy, Mari,' said Olav.

'I know, Olav, I know,' smiled back Mari.

'Mari, Mari are you all right?' A worried Julius was holding her hand. 'You fell from your chair and banged your head. Too much wine eh?'

'Did you follow me here Julius?' said Mari confusedly.

'I came to find you. Your mother told me where you had gone for the evening,' replied Julius.

'Has it been snowing?' questioned Mari.

'No, like I say you fell from your chair. I think I should get you home. I'll call a cab.'

'But I'm marrying Olav,' cried out Mari.

'Mari, you aren't marrying any Olav. You were supposed to be marrying me until we fell out, sort of. I see you still have the piece of paper in your hand that I sent over to your table earlier, saying that *it's all happening at 7pm Mari, through the main doors.* It's to be our engagement. Didn't you see me sitting in the corner? Look this is for you.' He offered her a diamond cluster ring he had in his pocket and as he did so, she saw her snowflake ring start to melt.

She screamed out, 'No, no I already have my engagement ring! Look Julius, look! Olav gave it to me!' and with that she got up and rushed for the main doors and pushed through them out into the drifting snow.

Olav was waiting in the sled.

'I love you Olav. You saved me from that dreaded dreary Christmas,' cried Mari.

'And I love you Mari. You saved me from being that eany-weany Helf helper.'

'Let's go before Julius finds us. I'll tell you about him later. No, on second thoughts, I don't want to talk about him anymore,' said Mari agitatedly.

'He won't see us,' replied Olav, 'The Dead Pan Arms is worlds away.' In the blink of an eye, they were away and heading for *The Way To The North.*

Julius ran after Mari and out of the doors of The Dead Pan Arms. As he stepped out into the dismal grey clouded night with scattered puddles of rain, he nearly tripped over a pair of ice skates. Then he saw in a dirty puddle Mari's wig of perfect curls, now unkempt and soggy. 'Mari, Mari,' Julius screamed. 'Come back. What's happened? Where are you? Marry me Mari. Mari, Mari, marry me Mari!' but his words were left hanging in the Christmas Eve drizzling, damp, dull air.

RETIREMENT PARTY
Moira Gibb

Frances sat perched on a chair in her glittery black dress with her perfect curls falling elegantly onto her shoulders. A whole party bustled around her. Hidden in the corner she gracefully sipped her wine, scanning the room for a familiar face. Why has she really bothered coming anyway? A whole bunch of pretentious strangers, slapping each other on the back, congratulating one another on pure hearsay. It had seemed such an excellent idea to try something new, but now it seemed so incredibly wrong. Honestly, what had possessed her to attend a . . . retirement party?

It wasn't any kind of a party, it was a retirement party, to celebrate with the person all the time they had been working for that company, it was after all since they had left school. It must have been 40 years.

Frances was new in town so Mary, Anne, Rose and Gemma had asked her to go. When Frances arrived and saw no sign of them, well, that happening made her feel uneasy.

Just as she was about to leave the party, Mary and the others had arrived. Frances asked, 'Why are you late?'

Mary answered, 'It took ages to start the car.'

Frances then said, 'I thought that you would be here before me tonight as it's my first time, I've been on my own all night, it couldn't be helped since nobody knows me. Still you're here now, that's the main thing, don't do it again.'

Mary said, 'We won't, now Frances, what do you want to drink?'

Frances replied, 'I'd like a Harvey's Bristol Cream please.'

Mary replied, 'Coming right up.'

After they had all had a few drinks, they all relaxed a bit, not to much, and thoroughly enjoyed themselves.

Now that Mary and the others were here, some men came over to talk to them, all very polite gentlemen who don't take advantage of women.

These men asked Mary, Frances, Anne, Rose and Gemma if they would like to go for a meal and a drink somewhere. All of them said they would like that. So off they went, had a lovely time then went dancing after that. Everyone had a whale of a time; they would all like to meet up again sometime.

THE PARTY
Keith F Lainton

She sat perched on a chair in her glittery black dress with her perfect curls falling elegantly onto her shoulders. A whole party bustled around her. Hidden in the corner she gracefully sipped her wine, scanning the room for a familiar face. Why has she really bothered coming anyway? A whole bunch of pretentious strangers, slapping each other on the back, congratulating one another on pure hearsay. It had seemed such an excellent idea to try something new, but now it seemed so incredibly wrong. Honestly, what had possessed her to attend . . . a dinner where she knew no one who would be there?

Patricia had phoned and made the whole evening sound like a really thrilling adventure, but where was Patricia? It was almost time for the dinner to be served and though Muriel worked with these people she was very new to the company and knew few of the guests.

Patricia and Rodney walked slowly towards their home. They had plenty of time to complete their walk; have their showers and get ready for the grand dinner they were invited to that evening at the home of the self-made millionaire who owned the company where Rod worked. As they went along they noticed a young, attractive and rather well dressed woman talking to two very tough looking men. Both Patricia and Rodney commented on the unusual mix.

'They can't be her boyfriends. That's for sure,' affirmed Pat.

'No, I'd be surprised if they're business colleagues either,' agreed Rod, 'though I suppose that depends on what sort of business he's in,' he added.

They walked on enjoying the pleasant sunshine. 'Don't suppose we'll get many more days like this,' Pat summed up both their thoughts as they arrived home.

Pat's old school friend, Emma was babysitting for Charlotte while Pat and Rod went to dinner. Emma had two children of her own and had been a favourite of Charlotte's ever since she had first babysat for them.

They arrived at Sir Victor's and Lady Pamela's house at 7.45. That was 15 minutes after the time stated on the invitation and 15 minutes before the meal would be served. Pat had met Sir Victor once but had never met his wife.

Immediately they arrived, their host had come over to greet them. He said how pleased he was to see them, thanked them for coming and said how well they both looked. 'And how is little Charlotte?' he enquired.

'Oh she is absolutely fine,' said Pat. 'She is growing so much I doubt you'd recognise her now.'

Sir Victor introduced them to two couples standing talking nearby and drifted off to rejoin a group on the other side of the room. Pat was so busy talking to their new acquaintances that she didn't even have time to think of looking at all the other dresses in the room. She had intended to do that as soon as she arrived. She was a little anxious about her dress. She knew how much Rod enjoyed working in Sir Victor's company and she had chosen her most flattering evening dress. 'It's all right for you men,' she had frowned as they were getting ready, 'you just hire a DJ and you are sure to be OK.'

As she said this, she noticed the woman they had seen earlier in the day - the woman having the conversation with the rather tough looking pair. As she leaned towards Rod to tell him, Pat realised that he too had noticed the intriguing woman.

At that moment Sir Victor rejoined them. 'Pat, I don't believe you have met my wife. Do come over and let me introduce you.'

Lady Pamela seemed very relaxed, Pat thought. She herself was always quite anxious before dinner guests actually started to eat - just in case the food went wrong.

'I hope we don't have one of these wretched burglaries that seem to be doing the rounds at the moment,' Lady Pamela commented.

Rob and Pat exchanged the sort of glance that couples, who understand the way each other think, sometimes exchange. Each knew the other was thinking of the woman they had seen earlier with her strange friends.

'Oh yes,' their host added by way of explanation. 'At a whole series of dinner parties there have been a number of thefts. Not large items taken. No signs of a break-in at any of them. Really looks as though someone invited has done it. Just sort of helped themselves. Unthinkable I know, but there it is.'

Dinner was announced and everyone walked through to the dining room. Rod and Pat both commented to each other afterwards at how well the table was set out. 'Did you see how the silver and the place mats and trays looked?' asked Pat.

'Yes, and how the light caught the sets of crystal glasses at everyone's setting,' agreed Rod.

The meal itself was excellent. Afterwards, when the party was having drinks in their hosts' large lounge, both of them agreed that as they ate their minds had been on the question of the intriguing woman.

'Could she be the thief?' whispered Pat.

'Yes and were the two men she was with her accomplices?' suggested Rod.

'Or could they be blackmailing her into taking stuff and handing it over to them?' considered Pat.

They agreed that they would make sure that they kept a close watch on the woman for the rest of the evening, concluding that before the meal there had been little opportunity for any theft in the room with so many people present, or at the dinner table itself.

'Well, we'll jolly well be sure that no opportunity occurs now,' determined Rod.

Two of Rod's immediate work associates came over to talk to them and they were soon deep in conversation about an incident which had happened at work the day before. Pat, however, never took her eyes off the woman in question and when her target got up and moved to leave the room, Pat made an excuse and followed. Pat saw the woman glance furtively behind her and then she slipped through a door into a room where none of the guests had been invited. Pat wondered what the best plan would be. *If I follow her in,* she thought, *any pretence at secrecy would be lost and if I burst in too soon she will simply say that she has taken a wrong turn and not have had time to take whatever it is she is after.* While she was deciding what to do, Pat heard the sound of a conversation through the door the woman had entered. As she listened Pat realised that though she could hear the woman's voice, she could hear the replies. *I wonder if one of those toughs has got in and they are planning what to steal?* thought Pat. Then it occurred to her that probably the woman was talking on a phone. Her small evening bag would easily conceal a mobile phone. *Perhaps she has been casing the joint,* thought Pat, lapsing into the kind of phrase she read in some of her favourite detective novels. I suppose she could easily be checking which items her accomplices would be able to fence. Pat moved nearer the door because the conversation was now very faint and she could no longer hear the actual words being said. The voice was still talking. 'Oh, what are they saying?' fretted Pat.

Just then the door from the lounge opened and Pat had to turn and walk back to avoid being caught eavesdropping at the door. As she entered the room she realised that there was a slight disturbance at the far end of the room. She also saw immediately that Rod was there and so she hurried to join him. She arrived just in time to hear their hostess saying that a jewelled cigarette case had been stolen. 'Neither of us actually smokes. It belonged to my father. It is quite valuable actually but apart from that it is of sentimental value. He took it everywhere with him. When I was a little girl he always let me hold it. I used to love to watch the light reflecting on it.' Lady Pamela was, understandably very distressed.

Pat immediately said, 'We think we know who the thief is.'

There was an instant silence in the room and Pat realised that everyone was looking at her.

'This afternoon we saw one of your guests here. In fact we were very surprised to see her when we came in. Anyway, Rob and I had a little conference and we decided to keep an eye on her, after you mentioned the robberies. I had just gone out but . . . ' she paused for a moment, wondering exactly how to explain to everyone that she thought she might have overheard part of a phone call that might possibly have some relevance. Suddenly it did not sound at all convincing.

Rod, who had beckoned Muriel to join them, continued from where Pat had let off, without the slightest pause ' . . . but, while Pat was out of the room we continued watching. Perhaps we could go somewhere private for a moment, Sir Victor?' he asked.

'Oh yes, of course.' Their host and hostess looked both alarmed and puzzled and they led Pat and Rod out, along the hall and, to Pat's surprise, into the very room that Pat had seen their quarry enter. No one was in the room now. Turning to them, Sir Victor said, 'Now, what on earth is all this?'

Pat felt slightly relieved to be out of sight and hearing of all the guests but still did not know how to make their total lack of real evidence sound adequate as a basis to accuse a fellow guest. However it was Rod who spoke. 'While Pat was out of the room Muriel and I kept watching and we saw, quite clearly the elderly lady in the long blue dress walk up to the table where the cigarette case was. She stopped and picked it up. I thought she was just admiring it, but no. She put it in her bag.'

For several seconds no one spoke. Only Rod was looking at Pat. If Sir Victor and his wife had looked they would have seen that her expression was just as surprised as theirs. The incident was handled very quietly. Sir Victor simply asked the old lady if she happened to have seen his wife's cigarette case. She opened her bag and said, very calmly, 'Oh is this it by any chance? I picked it up somewhere.'

Muriel, fearing that the lady had grown very forgetful, gushed, 'Some of her family could go round to her home. Her family could arrange for her to live with them.' However at that moment the woman that Pat and Rod had suspected entered the room.

'I am DS Hart,' she announced - producing her warrant card. 'We have been watching this one for a while but never had any evidence before.'

Three arrests later and many happy hosts received the unexpected but welcome return of valued treasures and the amazing series of thefts stopped and were never resumed. No one other than the six people in the room where the secret was revealed, ever knew the full truth.

Muriel came over and whispered to Pat, 'You were right, it really was a thrilling evening. I won't need the lift home you offered, thanks. George from accounts is taking me.'

'You know,' Rod's employer said to him the following week, 'we are really very grateful to you and Pat. You two should take this sort of thing up professionally.'

Rod told Pat about this next evening. 'I'd really love to do that,' replied Pat.

UNTITLED
Jean Bailey

She sat perched on a chair in her glittery black dress with her perfect curls falling elegantly onto her shoulders. A whole party bustled around her. Hidden in the corner she gracefully sipped her wine, scanning the room for a familiar face. Why has she really bothered coming anyway? A whole bunch of pretentious strangers, slapping each other on the back, congratulating each other on pure hearsay. It had seemed such an excellent idea to try something new, but now it seemed so incredibly wrong. Honestly, what had possessed her to attend a . . . function like this, it was not really her scene at all.

Suddenly one of the crowd moved near where she was sitting and the rest followed. They were fooling about when one of them knocked her elbow and her glass fell to the floor and the wine spilt down her dress. She was angry and flew at the guy who was very apologetic even to the point of offering to buy her a new dress. She said no.

'Then let me take you out to dinner,' he said. She looked into his pale blue eyes and said yes. He took her and introduced her to his friends. The evening turned out well and a year later the two were married.

She thought they were very happy and in love. When he worked all the time, he said it was for her he did it. When he came home with scent on, he said it was aftershave. She knew it wasn't. Red lipstick on his shirt he said was paint, she knew, of course, it wasn't.

One day she followed him to a friend's house and knocked the door. Her friend opened the door wearing a short flimsy night-dress. Her husband was coming downstairs adjusting his clothes. She flipped and started to run.

Back at the flat she plunged a kitchen knife into his clothes. She heard his car and ran down the stairs and waited behind the door. As the door opened she plunged the knife into him. The more he yelled, the more she plunged it into him, until he stopped. She then picked up the phone and gave herself up to the police.

She was sentenced to murder with intent, she hung herself with her tights in her cell.

SPARKLING WHITE
Margaret Webster

She sat perched on a chair in her glittery black dress with her perfect curls falling elegantly onto her shoulders. A whole party bustled around her. Hidden in the corner she gracefully sipped her wine, scanning the room for a familiar face. Why has she really bothered coming anyway? A whole bunch of pretentious strangers, slapping each other on the back, congratulating each other on pure hearsay. It had seemed such an excellent idea to try something new, but now it seemed so incredibly wrong. Honestly, what had possessed her to attend . . . a social evening organised by the local Badger Protection League.

She sipped again at the slightly sparkling white wine; she could taste the sugar, which had very obviously not had the opportunity to turn into alcohol. She shivered involuntarily; not due solely to the wine, because there was a slight draught caused by the open door to her left. It had been a pleasantly warm July day, but someone else had presumably found it as stifling as she did in this room and had sought a means of ventilation. She could make her escape through that door, if she was quick! Would anyone miss her? She was well hidden behind the two stocky gentlemen who had introduced themselves briefly as 'retired and making the most of it'. They were both then, onto their second glass of full-bodied red - that was the bold and elegantly written description of the wine box beside them.

'Grand news isn't it?' the craggier of the two men had said as she hovered by the table. 'This bypass being shifted to the other side of the woods,' He jiggled the knot of his canary yellow tie and smoothed his hand down the front of his pale blue checked shirt in fastidious mode.

Megan had barely twitched the muscles of her mouth in reply.

'Don't let's count chickens, and all that,' his companion reproached him, downing the remains of his wine. 'But why not?' he added jovially, the diamond-shaped patterns on his sweater bouncing over his rotund stomach. 'It's in the bag, sure as life. It's good to taste success.' In illustration of which, he'd siphoned himself off another glass of wine.

They'd both instantaneously forgotten that she was there, as they discussed the tactics employed in their campaign to change the proposal of a road through the lower fields, used - surprisingly enough, by the local badger sett.

Megan had retreated to the burgundy red upholstered chairs lined up by the wall and took no comfort from the light and fruity white wine she had been ceremoniously supplied with.

Where was Dan? He'd promised to meet her here by eight o'clock. How could he abandon her like this? Megan craned her neck to survey the room again. Her eyes met those of Norma Jewitt, postmistress and political activist for most of her sixty years. It was *she* who had enlisted Megan into this crusade. Signing her name on the petition handed to her across the counter had somehow activated her membership to the league. Norma now swept across the room, preceded by her triple strength perfume.

'Oh, how lovely to see you Maggie dear.'

'Megan,' Megan tried to correct her diplomatically as she stood up.

'Yes, yes. Come and meet some of the gang.' Norma took firm hold of her arm and propelled her into the centre of the room towards an herbaceous border of skirts and tops. 'This is Maggie. Now what *is* your surname? I should know really; it's my job after all to remember little details like that.' She laughed operatically. 'Anyway, Maggie has just moved into Avondale - on her own,' she mouthed at the group. 'So, we must make her feel welcome.' Norma introduced each of the four women in turn, but their names evaporated into the close atmosphere of the room.

'Ah, here is Squadron Leader Birkett. Can I leave you my dear? You're in safe hands with the girls.'

Megan rubbed at her bare arm, still imprinted with Norma's eager grip. 'My name is actually Megan. Megan Reilly.' She forced a smile. Four pairs of middle-aged eyes took in her black, halter neck dress.

'You look *very* pretty,' the woman at her right elbow said, obviously reiterating a point made in an earlier conversation.

'You might find our ways not as sophisticated as perhaps you're used to,' a tall, ash-blonde woman commented through a condescending smirk. 'Tish' - was that what Norma had said? The name summed her up perfectly.

'Does your hair curl naturally that way? I so envy anyone with nice hair.' The woman to her right tugged at her own grey-flecked and wispy mid-brown hair.

Someone rapped on a table to an accompaniment of tinkling glasses and a rendition of assorted coughs. Plenty of chiefs, but hardly an Indian in sight thought Megan.

'Well, it's almost official. I've just been told on good authority that we've won through the first phase.' Squadron Leader Birkett raised his glass of red wine. 'The Highway Commission has acknowledged our objections and proposals will go ahead for re-routing the bypass a mile west of Ripley Wood.' His voice rose to a crescendo as it was met by applause.

'Such sweet creatures.' The woman on Megan's right sighed. Megan frowned; who in this room was 'sweet'? 'I could watch them for hours. Usually do, when they cross through the bottom of my garden,' she giggled.

'Really Fran, you sentimentalise everything.' Tish pursed her lips. 'It's the principle that counts. We can't have some bureaucrat in London riding roughshod over us. Don't get me wrong - the wildlife is an important issue - but principles come first.'

'Let's toast ourselves on a job well done.' Norma Jewitt's rich voice rang out.

Full-bodied reds clinked with light and fruity whites.

'Let's not forget the badgers.' A man's throaty laugh hailed. Glasses chinked again.

'Badgers,' echoed and trailed around the room.

Megan looked down at her glass; perhaps the badgers would like to finish this for her? She'd never actually seen a live badger. Maybe she should visit Fran's garden. She'd heard that badgers could give you a rather nasty bite - like a few of the other locals! Dan was proud of her though; sticking up for animals. Animals were his passion, always had been, ever since he was a small boy. It was no surprise to anyone that he had become a vet, or that he had moved away from suburbia into the leafy lanes of the Cotswolds. It was a bit more of a surprise when Megan had followed him albeit to the next village, giving up her prestigious job running the modelling agency. It was all part of an image change, she told her family, settling down at last just as they had always wanted, and learning to appreciate the finer points of life. The madcap idea of joining the Badger Protection League was perhaps a bit extreme, even for her. Agreeing to 'pop in' at this party in the Country Club only emphasised her mistake. And the dress? Well, it wasn't for this lots' benefit. She was a neat size 12, so why not flaunt it? She twisted the gold ring on her left hand; she was still the same size as she had been when she married 30 years ago. She'd worn ivory satin then, so why black now? Black suited her, which was just as well, given her bereavement eighteen months ago. She drank off the remainder of the wine to ease the sudden swelling in her throat and shuddered.

'Ah, at last, Dan had arrived.'

'Sorry I'm late.' He kissed Megan on the cheek. 'Awkward patient,' he winked. 'Anyway, I'm here now to rescue you.'

Megan looked up into his vivid blue eyes. Six foot and growing more handsome every day with his sun-streaked blonde hair; she adored him. 'So, where are you taking me for dinner?'

'Somewhere very special, for a very special - and amazingly beautiful Mum, on her 50th birthday.'

Megan pulled at her, not altogether natural, curls. 'Shush! Don't give away *all* of my secrets - I'm saving them for the badgers.

HAPPENSTANCE
Margaret Green

She sat perched on a chair in her glittery black dress with her perfect curls falling elegantly onto her shoulders. A whole party bustled around her. Hidden in the corner she gracefully sipped her wine, scanning the room for a familiar face. Why has she really bothered coming anyway? A whole bunch of pretentious strangers, slapping each other on the back, congratulating each other on pure hearsay. It had seemed such an excellent idea to try something new, but now it seemed so incredibly wrong. Honestly, what had possessed her to attend . . . a wedding reception of complete strangers.

The only one familiar with the bride's parents had deserted her and now she wished she hadn't been persuaded to stay. She raised her glass intending to drain it then seek a means of escape, but a good sauternes deserved more respect. Paul would have enjoyed it too. Not just the wine but the evening itself. He loved the social scene. Any excuse and he was right there in the midst of it all. Tears veiled her lashes, and blinking rapidly, she reached for the wine. It was then she saw the man framing the doorway. There was something tangible in the knowing look he returned, almost as if he was thinking, *had they met somewhere?* but of course they hadn't. She would have remembered those rugged good looks, that splendid physique. Inexplicably she found herself blushing, and to cover her confusion, picked up her glass and drained the contents, then taking advantage of the enthusiastic welcome he was receiving, she slowly inched out of her seat, gathered her shawl, her bag, and the moment the band struck up, slipped away unnoticed.

Outside, she crossed the deserted promenade, removed her shoes, and walked down the sloping ramp onto the firm, damp sands the outgoing tide had left behind. Stretching before her the beach glistened smoothly, except for the elongated chevron ridges, a scattering of shells and dark tangles of seaweed. The westering July sun had turned the ocean to flame, and as she gazed at the changing scene, a light mist began to form over the restless suck and draw of the cream-topped rollers. Except for the wheeling crying gulls, the silence was complete and she found the solitude most comforting. Paul had loved this place. Here, they strolled of an evening, her arm tucked snugly in his, each intent on their thoughts more often than not. Hers on domestic affairs, her little business, or what to wear for some future occasion, and he, always with an eye on advancement would pause, take in the view, heave an appreciative sigh and elaborate on some newly conceived scheme that even as he spoke, would realise the futility of it, and with a lopsided grin he'd say, 'Well perhaps not.' She found his boyish swing from eagerness to doubt so appealing, and reaching for him would kiss him soundly.

Loving him in death as much as in life she called out, weeping brokenly, 'Oh God! Help me. I can't bear this pain,' then turning on her heel, leaving a swirling imprint in the sand, retraced her steps.

The stranger on the jetty watched and waited. A silver moon had replaced the sun, and it wasn't until she arrived within a few feet, that she saw him. 'You are upset,' he said gently, his voice falling pleasantly between them. 'I'd like to help if I can,' but she had nothing to say, and sensing her reticence, he went on. 'I've a feeling we've met, yet I can't remember where. I'm Noel Bradbury, does that ring a bell?'

In the moonlight her teeth flashed white and even as she smiled.

'Verna Fouché!'

'You were my husband's broker.'

He accepted her proffered hand saying, 'The casino owner!'

She nodded.

'Why did you leave?

'I felt overcome by the crowd. I recognised no one. Your dealings were with Paul's solicitor and accountant. Perhaps you saw me at the funeral, I'm afraid I wasn't very au-fait that day.'

'Perfectly understandable, only I remember seeing you. I'm terribly sorry. How long ago is it - three, four years?

'Nearly five,' her lips trembled, 'since his plane disappeared below the waves, the day after my twenty-seventh birthday. God, what a waste. If only I had been with him I wouldn't be hurting now.' She bent to put on her shoes, then, straightening up, scanned the house on the clifftop. Its white walls held a ghostly aura, but the windows gleamed brightly at the smiling moon. 'I'm tempted to sell,' she spoke dully, 'only Paul had it built for us. You know he is still there tunefully singing and whistling through the empty rooms.' She began crying in earnest again, so he held her face, and thumbed away the tears before producing a clean handkerchief.

He wanted to hold her, to kiss away her grief, only he couldn't risk being rebuffed so advised instead. 'You should take a holiday. Paul's family will welcome you. The sun seeking hordes won't have invaded Le Touquet yet, why don't you go?'

Then, taking her hand, he walked her to the green Jaguar parked at the kerb. Something else, he thought, she couldn't let go. 'I can't face going anywhere,' she blew her nose. 'Thanks for this,' she held up the soggy handkerchief. 'I'll wash it and return it to your office.'

'I've got a better idea,' he grinned. 'Have dinner with me tomorrow.'

She looked momentarily startled, then to his delight, smilingly accepted.

'Noel,' someone called from outside the hotel. 'What the devil are you doing? Come on old chap, you're missing the fun.'

'Won't you join us?' he asked waving a hand of assent, but she only shook her head.

'Tomorrow then,' he held her hand. 'I'll call for you, say six thirty?'

'Fine,' was all she said.

Noel drove the Volvo T5 along Marine Parade and, climbing ever upward, arrived at the house aptly named 'Ocean View'.

'That's some hill,' he laughed, meeting Verna in the recessed colonnaded entrance.

'Oh,' her smile reached her eyes, 'I assumed you would know the easier route. If you come again you must take the road at the end of the esplanade, it's much less steep.'

'We live and learn,' he said, amusement drawing up his lips as he followed her across the wide square hall into the rectangular drawing room, with its panoramic view of the sea.

'A drink?' she asked.

'A small whisky and soda, remember, I'm driving,' he answered, adding, 'thanks,' when she handed it to him. 'I love your dress,' he grinned appreciatively. 'Green suits you. It matches your eyes.'

'Paul . . . ' She began than shrugged. 'No, I promised myself I would keep him out of tonight's conversation. I'm so glad you like it.'

He wandered over to the window and she thought, *he's relieved,* and respected him the more for it.

He took her to a cosy little inn on the edge of Keystone Bay that held no memories of Paul. She wondered if he had known, but determined to keep her word, she invited him to talk about himself.

'Well,' he leaned his elbows on the table, and gazing directly at her went on, 'I live with my parents.' She laughed, more out of glee than scorn, but he simply indulged her and continued. 'They moved here when I was still at Oxford. It seemed natural that I should join them. I've never married. I have a sister in America. She's a research chemist. That's about it really.'

There were many such evenings as they slowly drew together. One time she surprised him by saying she never accepted any money from Paul, never entered his casinos. 'But how have you managed, did Paul settle accounts or something?'

'No, nothing like that,' she told him. 'I have a shop. I sell flowers, my dad bought it for me. I take my living expenses out of the profits.'

'Where do you sell your flowers?'

'On Brook Street, it's called The Rose Bowl.'

'I've never seen you in there.'

She smiled and wondered if her admiration for him showed, but he remained seemingly unaware. So she said, 'I employ two girls. I spend my time making up orders, I never go out front.'

One evening in October he took her hand saying apologetically, 'I have to go to Geneva, come with me please?' He saw the guarded look and added quickly, 'No strings, honest. I've grown used to you. I like having you around.'

She gazed into his expressive cornflower blue eyes and, having come close to loving him, felt secure in saying, 'You don't have to burden yourself out of pity you know.'

He looked more taken aback than hurt and recovering quickly went on. 'These past weeks you've brought new meaning into my life. I'm more than halfway to loving you. All I need is a little encouragement. I want you to come. I shall be very unhappy if you say no.' Then smilingly, 'Come on, be a devil, take a chance.'

It surprised no one, when on their return at Christmas, they announced their engagement and in the spring when the first visitors arrived at Keystone Bay, they were just in time to see a happy couple and their guests entering the promenade hotel.

THE SÉANCE
Hilarie Grinnell

She sat perched on a chair in her glittery black dress with her perfect curls falling elegantly onto her shoulders. A whole party bustled around her. Hidden in the corner she gracefully sipped her wine, scanning the room for a familiar face. Why has she really bothered coming anyway? A whole bunch of pretentious strangers, slapping each other on the back, congratulating each other on pure hearsay. It had seemed such an excellent idea to try something new, but now it seemed so incredibly wrong. Honestly, what had possessed her to attend a . . . séance like this? Christina Francis was wondering.

Not like a business meeting - this mainly consisted of people who wanted to get in touch with those who have passed away. A spiritualistic meeting of all kinds of people, from different backgrounds and different nationalities.

The prime figure was a white man of about forty, tall with dark brown hair and magnetic eyes. His name was Adam Sanderson. Very magnetic personality and attractive to women, Adam began the meeting. He stood up to speak. At the top end of the large drawing room was an elevated floor with a microphone standing in the middle of it. He opened his talk, thanking all the people who had come from miles around, for attending the meeting. Then he started talking about someone from the spirit life (which Christina thought was all wrong). All the people in the room were wanting to get through to someone who had passed over.

After a while a plump Chinese woman was given a message, from her husband who had died three years previously. She was grateful.

After one hour had passed, Adam Sanderson brought his part of the meeting to a close, and some of the audience left, then the people who had stayed behind walked over to a large round table and sat around it. Christina did not want to join in, so she continued to sit in the leather chair nearest the door and observed everything that was going on. It seemed that there were many keen people who wanted to get in touch with the spirit world. Christina found it somehow disturbing, and as an onlooker, she watched and waited, but did not want to participate. As she sipped her red wine the room turned cold, and she shuddered. *Why had she come to this séance?* she wondered. Cajoled by a friend, Anna

Davidson, she had accepted out of curiosity more than anything else. Then the lights were dimmed, and Christina shrank back into the leather chair even more.

A dark haired woman called Maria Cavallero, an Italian, proceeded with the séance. She started her meeting with a little boy who had died, wanting to get a message to his mother. It seemed the child had been killed in a motor accident and needed to communicate to the mother not to be worried, that he was all right.

Christina was not at all sure, she had come to the right place, since she was a Christian and spiritualism was not correct where she had come from. Her father had been a priest all of her life, and her mother and herself had been educated religiously not to interfere with spiritualism! She spoke quietly to her friend indicating that she would stay for a while longer, but she felt this meeting was not the right thing for her. Then Miss Cavallero stated there was somebody sitting at the circular table who had been ill with cancer, but had been given hospital treatment and as 'all clear' now. She indicated to a young woman with blonde hair and creamy complexion. This lady, was a secretary to a law firm, but became tearful as she realised Miss Cavallero was speaking about her. The lady's name was Clare Jennings, but she seemed relieved that her illness was now gone.

Then an old man of about seventy, asked Miss Cavallero, if she could get a message through to his beloved wife who had passed away two years previously. She was not successful for some reason, and the old man was disappointed.

Christina thought there were so many people, who had lost someone through illness or motor accidents, and their only hope of contacting the person was through this method of meeting. She still did not approve though. Her years being spent as a vicar's daughter had taught her that spiritualism was interfering with another world - one that was best to leave alone.

However, the meeting carried on for another hour. Many people had been given solace for contacting someone they had lost, through illness. A woman of about forty, with lovely white hair, but had poor eyesight, was told by Miss Cavallero that she would see better again and not lose her sight. Sara Carter felt so happy at hearing this, she promptly started to cry tears of joyfulness. She was quite overcome, as she had to put up with a lot of trouble over her poor eyesight. It had impeded her lifestyle for many years, and she had not been able to do all the things she wanted to do, like drive a car.

Christina had finished her glass of wine and was sipping slowly her second refill. She was not sure whether this meeting was wrong or based on faith healing. She talked quietly to her friend, who was sitting near to her. 'I'm not sure about all this healing, not sure at all,' she admitted to Anna.

'Well it has been an experience that you will never forget!' Anna replied.

'Faith healing is all right if it's used constructively to help people, but I find all this spiritualism stuff slightly unbelievable.' Christina was adamant. 'And it is against everything that I have been brought up to find acceptable.'

'We can go soon, when this Italian lady has finished the meeting, and then you will know not to come here again, as it has made you so uncomfortable,' Anna said in her caring manner.

Christina watched and waited. Never had she felt so disorientated. She did not want to come to a spiritual meeting again - it had been an odd experience for her, although maybe beneficial for others.

Maria Cavallero sensed disapproval from behind her. She looked up and saw Christina. She then proceeded to give a talk on 'mediums', claiming that people could be sceptical if they wished, but how much good that mediums do. Helping police in their enquiries with criminals etcetera, and aiding the police catch murderers. Christina thought about it, and realised that she had led a very protected life, from the outside world, and in many ways this was not a good thing.

So finally, Anna and Christina stayed and listened, trying not to be sceptical. Miss Cavallero then said there was a girl in the room with a bone disease, but she emphasised that this teenage girl was going to recover and become strong again. The girl had long red hair, and she stood up from sitting position, and thanked Miss Cavallero for giving her back her faith - because she had been so weak, her legs had not worked for some time. The meeting was over now, and people began to disperse from the large round table. Everyone was satisfied with the outcome - especially those people who had been helped. Even Anna and Christina were feeling better about the meeting now.

They decided they would go out for something to eat, at the little Indian restaurant round the other side of the square. London was always busy, but this evening the hustle and bustle had died down temporarily, and both girls were feeling hungry. When they arrived at the restaurant, they ordered quickly, so they would not have to wait too long for the food.

They both eat hungrily and enjoyed the meal immensely! Christina felt good - all her apprehension of the meeting had gone away, and Anna felt relieved too, so they drank some more wine with their food.

An hour later, they both took a taxi to go home. Anna was staying as a guest, at Christina's house in Bayswater. It had been a very eventful evening - one that they would not forget for many years to come.

A LIFETIME TO REMEMBER
Vera Parsonage

She sat perched on a chair in her glittery black dress with her perfect curls falling elegantly onto her shoulders. A whole party bustled around her. Hidden in the corner she gracefully sipped her wine, scanning the room for a familiar face. Why has she really bothered coming anyway? A whole bunch of pretentious strangers, slapping each other on the back, congratulating each other on pure hearsay. It had seemed such an excellent idea to try something new, but now it seemed so incredibly wrong. Honestly, what had possessed her to attend . . . a gathering of strangers, far beyond her league.

Linda was nineteen when she left college to take her place in university, the brains of a family of five children, her father owning a small grocery store in a small village. She had never mixed with the elite, and had never been away from home before, therefore she was very vulnerable, and very lonely. Her digs didn't give her the comfort of her home, being only a one room bedsit, shared with another student. She missed her family, Sue was her only friend. Her flatmate came from a very different background, her father being a doctor. Sue had many friends. The party was one of many events.

Gazing before the mirror, she felt her dress suitable to mix with the rest. Once there she felt terrible alone. Someone handed her a glass of wine then left her. She was just about to call it a day and walk out when she noticed a tall, fair haired man approach. He reminded her of a Greek god, and was dumbfounded when he spoke to her. His language wasn't like the rest of the students - French or maybe German. His smile was captivating. 'May I offer you a drink?' he asked.

She had never seen him about, and she had to wonder where he had come from. He placed his glass in front of her, and removed her empty one. Time passed in an uncanny way.

She had a warm, dizzy feeling which she had never felt before. He called himself Carl, a student exchange from Holland, studying English.

Taking her arm he helped her to the entrance, and she felt sure that the drink had given her this strange feeling. She hung onto the stone statue edging the steps, then passed out.

Time must have gone, she opened her eyes to find herself in a van, covered in a small thin blanket, and not very clean. Her thin jacket was

47

not sufficient to protect her enough to keep her warm. Coming to her senses, she started to scream, which ended with a slap across the face. Her last drink must have been spiked. The van began to slow up and then came to a halt. She was roughly dragged out of the van to find herself at a small jetty, and a boat standing by. It was obvious that they were going to sail out to sea.

She was pushed into the boat and into a cabin with just one porthole. A tear trickled down her cheek. She could hear footsteps above and strange voices in a foreign language. The door was opened by a rough looking man, who would have done justice to a wash and shave. He handed her a cracked cup which hardly resembled coffee, and placed a tin plate on the floor with two bread rolls spread with something that hardly resembled butter. Linda was hungry and too weak to refuse. She managed to look through the porthole. A small fishing boat sailed past, but it was impossible to draw their attention. Someone turned the key of the door and another girl was pushed inside. She slid across the floor with a mouthful of abuse. Her Cockney accent didn't become her looks, which were not enhanced with her make-up.

Swearing, she threw her shoe at the locked door. 'Bastard, they promised me my own apartment in Paris and as many clients as I wanted, I was to be rich. What did they offer you?'

Linda didn't quite understand what she meant, but she had her own idea. They were heading for a brothel in France, and this girl knew all the answers.

It was beginning to get dark. A small light gave them little comfort. Linda couldn't stem her tears. 'Why am I here?' she asked herself.

Her companion was cynical. 'You came to get rich,' she replied.

'I didn't choose to be here,' she sobbed, 'I was kidnapped.'

Her companion laughed, 'I will be rich, and so will you when we reach France.'

'France!' Linda sobbed, 'I don't have reason to go to France.'

The other girl roared out laughing, 'How naive you are.'

As time passed the sea became rough. All they could do was to snuggle together beneath the blanket.

It was breaking daylight when they came to their senses. Looking through the porthole they could see a stretch of land, to which they sailed past heading for a sandy patch hidden from the commercial landing.

A burly man took the arm of both girls and led them to a waiting van. Roughly they were thrown inside. They must have travelled a few hours before they came to a halt.

The two girls were pulled out. They stood for a moment taking note of where they were, standing on the bank of a canal. A few cyclists whistled as they past, in fact most of the passers by were riding bikes. They seemed to be in a country village, a few miles from Belgium. The girls were taken to a nearby seat and told to wait. The captor returned to the van and drove off. Within minutes a car drove up at a frightening speed and demanded the girls to get in. They dare not disobey, he had a revolver in one hand, with the other on the steering wheel, driving at a frightening speed through a town that seemed to be full of trams and people. He came to a large house and lifted the brass knocker. The door was opened by a portly woman in a dress that seemed too short for her age.

'Come in dears,' she said taking the arm of each girl. Her accent was English, but to Linda her smile was false. She led them into the hallway into the most beautiful parlour Linda had ever seen, beckoning them to sit down on a red, plush couch behind two marble tables. Picking up a bell, she rang it and in walked a girl with a tray of food. The girls were hungry and ate the food with relish.

'This is where you will work,' the woman said leading each to a room. That was the last she saw of the other girl, she had reached her destination, and was prepared to work for Madam. Linda just wanted to get back home. Behind the door was a shower and she was tempted.

Linda hadn't wiped herself dry when there was a terrific bang as the door burst open, and two uniform officers burst in. She grabbed at her clothes. Swiftly they bundled her into a police car. An English girl in a French brothel didn't make sense. She spent the night in a police cell.

The morning brought a British investigator. Her statement helped them to catch the men who brought the girls over.

After the summer break she returned to college to receive the results of the exam. At the end of the term they got the results. Linda hadn't done too well, and her misery grew as the days went by.

The girl with the lovely, enchanting curls took a sip from the half empty glass she felt so much alone. It was the end of term, she finished her wine and left for her dismal room, her suitcase was under the bed. At that moment she made a snap decision. Emptying her drawer, she bundled her belongings into her suitcase and snapped down the lid. By the time her flatmate came in she was ready to leave.

Next morning she was on the train heading for home. Her father was puzzled as to why she had left, but college wasn't for her.

She worked in the little grocer's shop with its familiar smells - home baked bread, and bacon. She was a disappointment to her father, but it was happiness to her.

She never told of her kidnapping. The police came round to ask questions and her father learnt the whole story.

The years passed and as her father grew old, he died. This was her life - married to the son's owner of the confectioner's next door. The two shops joined and turned into a flourishing supermarket. Linda had no reason to look back, in a strange way she was grateful of her unusual experiences, with a lifetime to remember.

THE PARTY
Colin Zarhett

She sat perched on a chair in her glittery black dress with her perfect curls falling elegantly onto her shoulders. A whole party bustled around her. Hidden in the corner she gracefully sipped her wine, scanning the room for a familiar face. Why has she really bothered coming anyway? A whole bunch of pretentious strangers, slapping each other on the back, congratulating each other on pure hearsay. It had seemed such an excellent idea to try something new, but now it seemed so incredibly wrong. Honestly, what had possessed her to attend . . . a party with coke heads, drunks and butt heads . . . it all seemed surreal anyway.

Helen moved from the backside of the room. She attracted a lot of stares from old men and young men, and cold fish eye glares from their women partners. Helen was proud of the reaction she was receiving from the men in attendance at the party and was secretly elated that her feminine attributes were in full bloom.

Sir Arthur Croyden was probably the first and only person who could see the hidden anguish on her face. The party kept going with back-slapping and the clink of ice cubes tinkling. It all seemed unreal. Sir Arthur noticed an empty chair next to Helen. 'I believe, that the party is weakening,' he said to Helen. With steel blue eyes Helen stared at him. She almost dropped her glass. It seemed like she was trying to give him a message. Sir Arthur stiffly answered her stare with, 'Madam, you may have discovered the answer to the lad's problems.'

Helen looked like she understood his cryptic remark but wondered how he could have known that the only reason she was there was to solicit funds from these *stuff shirts* for Billy Bush's release from jail. She thought that she had been diplomatic in her solicitations - approaching only a few of her elite friends.

Before she knew it the party was over only the *hangers on* were still there. Sir Arthur looked around - empty glasses, partially filled glasses and ashtrays filled brimming with cigarette butts. With this mental picture playing over and over Sir Arthur made his way down the driveway and waited on his car - the valet was carefully engineering his Bentley to him. And before he knew it he was safely home, at his mansion, Bellemor. He stared into the fire. The fireplace was sending heat to all of the library. Sir Arthur was feeling relaxed. He sat his glass down on the coffee table. With a great sigh of relief, he sat back down in his favourite chair and his eyelids became heavy with sleep. Sir Arthur's dream machine went into overdrive. He dreamt of Helen. Her passion was extraordinary. They melted into one ball of quivering flesh . . . but only in his dreams.

WRITING CHALLENGE
Robert Henry Lonsdale

She sat perched on a chair in her glittery black dress with her perfect curls falling elegantly onto her shoulders. A whole party bustled around her. Hidden in the corner she gracefully sipped her wine, scanning the room for a familiar face. Why has she really bothered coming anyway? A whole bunch of pretentious strangers, slapping each other on the back, congratulating each other on pure hearsay. It had seemed such an excellent idea to try something new, but now it seemed so incredibly wrong. Honestly, what had possessed her to attend . . . such a dismal party to celebrate the release from prison of Jeffrey Archer.

If only she had let the police deal with the burglar they had caught absolutely red handed breaking into her house, as they had pleaded with her to do. But, oh no, all the streams of burgling crocodile tears had tweaked her open heart-strings and she had to be the compassionate woman, she had to be the new shining star in the endless galaxy of offender reform.

Live and let live she argued. He's learnt his lesson and we have to respond to that, so just give him a severe caution and we'll put an end to the matter.

'Very commendable,' the policeman said, 'but believe me, you will be sorry,' he added with his tongue bursting through his cheek.

The grateful burglar knew he had been extremely lucky to keep his liberty. 'Thank you kind lady,' he grovelled, 'you've got all your valuables back and I can promise you that I will be going straight from now on, and as a token of my gratitude I want you to accept this ticket which is an invitation to the Jeffrey Archer release from prison party. I won it in the bran tub draw while we were banged up together.'

So, here she is, seated alone with her thoughts, slowly sipping wine which she doesn't like anyway. Suddenly, an unfamiliar, brusque voice shattered her thoughts and brought her tumbling back into reality. 'On your own darling,' the voice enquired.

'Yes, yes I am,' she said sheepishly. The unknown man came closer to her. She didn't like the look of him. He reminded her of Jack Elam, the actor who always played the part of the slime-ball bad buy in western films.

'I'm taking orders,' the stranger asked, 'can I get you anything?'

She suddenly felt relaxed he wasn't as bad as she first thought. 'Yes, I'd like to try a Bacardi Breezer please.'

The man burst out laughing and the cigar he was smoking shot out of his mouth and landed amidst a flurry of sparks onto the plush carpet. He then trod on the cinder end with the sole of his shoe and ground the cigar into dust. 'Nawwww,' he drawled, 'I'm taking orders for tellies, fridges, any electrical goods, I have a contact at the factory you see.'

She felt completely stupid and immediately wished for an alien spaceship to arrive and beam her up to anywhere. 'Oh! I see . . . no, no, there's nothing I require thank you.'

The man was still laughing. 'If you do,' he said half heartedly, as he walked away from her, 'Bacardi Breezer, you know where I am.'

Oh dear, here she is once again alone with her ever wandering thoughts when her attention is attracted to a loud thumping noise now taking place at the far end of the large room. A red faced rotund man is standing behind a dinner table banging the table top with his tightly clenched fist causing all the cutlery and crockery to bounce about precariously.

'Ladies and gentlemen!' he bellows, 'it gives me great pleasure to welcome our guest of honour . . . Mr Jeffrey Archerrrrrr!'

The packed room then erupts into a cascade of shouting and clapping which increased in intensity when himself stepped sprightly onto a small podium situated in front of the dining table. His face was swathed in a broad smile and his outstretched arms reached out towards his noisy audience. 'Friends, believe me when I say . . . '

Before he uttered another word, 'Time for me to go,' she said to herself.

Yes, she had thought it would be an excellent idea to try something new and for her the party had been something of a surprise, but in truth she had attended the function mainly in the hope of meeting somebody rich and famous who would sweep her totally off her dainty size four feet and fly her straight to paradise in a private jet where they would both live happily ever after. She now realised however, that hope was never going to happen here and she also knew she wanted nothing more to do with this party.

So, without further ado she slipped deftly from her chair and headed straight for the exit. 'Can I have my coat please?' she said to a scantily clad maid.

'Do me a favour,' the indignant maid retorted angrily, 'I'm not a maid! I'm part of the entertainment!'

She forgot about collecting her coat and left the building never to return.

CLASS PREJUDICE
Michael N McKimm

She sat perched on a chair in her glittery black dress with her perfect curls falling elegantly onto her shoulders. A whole party bustled around her. Hidden in the corner she gracefully sipped her wine, scanning the room for a familiar face. Why has she really bothered coming anyway? A whole bunch of pretentious strangers, slapping each other on the back, congratulating each other on pure hearsay. It had seemed such an excellent idea to try something new, but now it seemed so incredibly wrong. Honestly, what had possessed her to attend . . . the chamber's annual dinner and dance.

Rachael's thoughts were suddenly interrupted. 'Excuse me love, you look lonely, and the wife and me thought you might like to join us?'

Rachael looked up from her glass, smothering her instinct to admonish the stranger for his patronising remark. Her indignation subsided quickly as she realised from his uneasiness that this was probably not his idea. 'No thank you Mr ah . . . '

'Watkins love, Clive Watkins, chairman of Watkins and Cooper Construction, and this is the wife, Shirley,'

Rachael followed Watkins' gesture, stifling an involuntary gasp as she caught sight of the descending apparition.

'Please to meet you hy'm sure,' said Mrs Watkins grasping Rachael's hand and shaking it vigorously. 'And what's your name dear?' she said smiling through huge red lips thickly covered with scarlet lip gloss, that matched the colour of her hair. 'She's lost her tongue I fink Clive,' she continued.

'Oh, I'm sorry, I'm Rachael Tompkinson,' said Rachael mesmerised by the woman in the tightest and shortest dress she had ever seen, with a plunging neckline that revealed a cavernous cleavage.

'I said to Clive we haven't seen you here before, or at any of the meetings. What is it you do then Rachael?'

'I own the Roland Gallery and Coffee Shop in Membery's Passage.'

'Oh, that sounds nice Clive, donnit, of course Clive likes 'is paintings don't you Clive?'

'Yes,' replied Clive, his neck and cheeks becoming flushed with embarrassment.

'Tell me Mr Watkins, what is it you paint?' asked Rachael, hoping to deflect the attentions of Mrs Watkins.

'I've always painted, ever since I was a . . . '

'Tell her about goin' to art college then Clivee,' interrupted Mrs Watkins.

'You went to art college?' asked Rachael.

'Yes, I went to the Bath College of Art when it was in Sydney Place,' replied Clive.

'Did you graduate, Mr Watkins?' asked Rachael, sitting up on her stool, her irritation subsiding, at what a moment ago was unwanted attention.

'Oh yeah, I ah got a two-one in Fine Art.'

''E's ever so proud of 'is degree, 'e's framed it, an' 'ung it up in 'is, what's it called Clivee?'

'Studio Shirley, you ought to know by now.'

'You have your own studio, Mr Watkins?' enquired Rachael.

'Yes, I built it in one of the outbuildings that we got with the house.'

'And we've got a pool with a covered roof and some 'orses, and . . . '

'Please Shirley,' said Clive, his voice becoming irritated, 'Mrs Tompkinson isn't interested in all of that stuff.'

'But didn't you say you were the chairman of a construction company?' asked Rachel.

'Cooee! Look there's Norma and Tom Wharton and Tom's brother,' called out Shirley. 'Do you mind if I go into the bar wiv them Cliveee? I'm dying for a Guiness.'

'No! Please go over, I'll join you later,' replied Clive.

'Okay,' said Shirley as she whispered into Clive's ear.

Rachel had sat bolt upright on her seat, leaning forward, eager to hear more about this unexpected introduction.

'Yeah, I'm the chairman, as I said.'

'But how did you do a Fine Art degree?' asked Rachael, running her hand through her hair.

'I've always enjoyed the arts, and I have always drawn and painted since I could hold a brush or a pencil. My father had the building business handed down to him from his father and he wanted me to follow him in turn.'

'But how did you manage to do your degree?' asked Rachael, warming to this more than one, faceted man.

'I did well at school, especially in art and by the time I was sixteen I was determined to go to college to further my interests and gain some qualifications.'

'Well I'd say you certainly did that.' said Rachael.

'It wasn't easy, you see my father insisted that I complete an apprenticeship as a Mason, and then he would pay for me to go to college. So I did a four year apprenticeship and then went to Bath College of Art.'

'Why didn't you go away from Bath to have the whole experience of student life?' Asked Rachael.

'The kids.'

'What do you mean, the kids. Oh do you mean you had a child by then?'

'Two! Shirley and me were going together since we were fifteen. We got married on her seventeenth birthday, she was five months pregnant, I'm six months older.'

'So how do you find time for painting, Mr Watkins?'

'Call me Clive, everybody calls me Clive, I've never been interested in formality.'

'Okay Clive, so tell me.'

'I work in the mornings, either with the Banker Masons in the workshop, which I really love. Or in the office which I don't like, but I have to oversee the business. But we are really lucky because the girls, we have five girls, all work for the company.'

'Five girls, what do they do?'

'They all have degrees. Jane is a lawyer, Paula is an accountant, June is a chartered surveyor. Olivia and Louise have language degrees and they are in sales and customer relations.'

'So this arrangement gives you the time to paint. Now Clive tell me what you paint?'

'Portraits and landscapes, always in oils and always impasto, the landscapes are often painted outside.'

'That's really interesting Clive, many of the paintings in my gallery are of that genre. We have an artist called Keith Fielden who is a prolific painter and we are lucky to be able to sell his work. Do you know of him?'

'Yes I have heard of him Rachael, but I believe he is quite reclusive.'

'He is, he only sells through his agent, Jeremy Anderson, who was supposed to come here tonight with me. He telephoned ten minutes after he was supposed to pick me up to say he was in a traffic jam on the M4.'

'So that's why you're here on your own?'

'Yes, and I was pretty well fed up when you came to my rescue.'

'Shirley picked up on that,' said Clive with a smile. 'She has an amazing ability to be able to know what someone is feeling.'

'You seem so different, you and Shirley I mean!' said Rachael in a successful attempt to get Clive to tell more.

'Shirley, ah Shirley is not what you would think she is from tonight's short introduction. She is very interested in the performing arts and is a talented actress and a singer.'

Rachael's face contorted as she tried to suppress an indulgent grin.

Clive smiled at her, saying, 'I think you will find out when we have the entertainment after dinner.'

'But that's from the Fairwood Light Operatic Ensemble.'

'Yes, that's right,' replied Clive.

'Oh look, there's Jeremy Anderson' gasped Rachael with a beaming smile that revealed the most beautiful set of glistening white teeth. Jeremy caught her eye from across the room and made his way through the throng.

'Hello Rachael, I'm so sorry about letting you down like that. I left in plenty of time, but there was an accident.' Jeremy turned and grasped Clive's hand, shaking it vigorously.

'Hello Clive old son, how are you?'

'Fine thanks Jeremy.'

'Well you two seem to have introduced yourselves,' questioned Rachael.

'We met at college,' said both men simultaneously and began laughing. *As though at some secret!* thought Rachael.

'What's Shirley dressed as tonight Clive?' asked Jeremy. Clive felt Rachael's eyes searching his own, her mouth opened as if to ask a question and stayed slightly open for a few seconds. At this Jeremy said, ' Clive you haven't told Rachael have you?'

'Told me what?' cried Rachael.

'He hasn't told you about Shirley being a member of the Northleach Natural Theatre Company, has he Rachael?'

'No, what is the Northleach Natural whatever?' asked Rachael with her voice raised in bewilderment.

'It's an Amateur Dramatic Society whose members appear in public as another personae, or as an animal.'

The three turned to see Shirley, who had given the answer. She wore a long flowing turquoise gown and the red wig - gone. Her black hair was swept up from the nape of her neck and showered a mass of curls over her forehead. She was the most beautiful woman in the room.

Rachael stared in disbelief, as Shirley placed her arms around her and kissed her cheek.

'Please forgive me Rachael, you see we wanted to make sure that you were without class prejudice.' said Shirley.

'Class prejudice. What do you mean?' said Rachael as Shirley, Clive and Jeremy stood smiling at her.

'There's someone who I want you to meet tonight Rachael, who would not have agreed to meet you if you had shown any class prejudice.'

Rachael turned to Clive and Shirley.

'You knew who I was all the time,' she stammered.

'Oh yes, all three of them did Rachael,' smiled Jeremy.

'Three of them, what three of them Jeremy? Jeremy what is going on?' cried Rachael, her voice rising higher. Jeremy gestured as he spoke.

'Clive Watkins and Shirley Watkins,' and then he raised his arm in a circle and brought it back to Clive, 'and Keith Fielden, whose paintings you exhibit and sell.'

Rachael's face turned white with shock. 'Clive, you are Keith Fielden, whose work I've admired and sold in Bath and London, and whom I've never had the good fortune to meet?'

'Yes I am indeed,' said Clive, grasping her hand and kissing her lightly on the cheek.

'Welcome Rachael, to our inner circle, you must never divulge my true identity. It is this anonymity that allows me the tranquillity that is vital to my inspiration. Come Rachael, you and Jeremy are sitting with Shirley and me and our five daughters, whose portraits you sell in your gallery.'

Rachael turned to see the five young women with their mother's inherited beauty, who had gathered silently behind her. Those faces that she knew so well, but who's identities had been a mystery.

MURDER, NO MYSTERY
Pamela Robson

She sat perched on a chair in her glittery black dress with her perfect curls falling elegantly onto her shoulders. A whole party bustled around her. Hidden in the corner she gracefully sipped her wine, scanning the room for a familiar face. Why has she really bothered coming anyway? A whole bunch of pretentious strangers, slapping each other on the back, congratulating each other on pure hearsay. It had seemed such an excellent idea to try something new, but now it seemed so incredibly wrong. Honestly, what had possessed her to attend . . . a murder mystery weekend?

Catherine had only been temping at Carter and Co for a mere three weeks, but she still qualified for a place on their team-building exercise of a murder mystery weekend. Not least of all because she let it slip that she was not currently in a relationship and the highlight of her Saturday was usually a pizza and video, topped off with a tub of Carte D'or. The unmarried career women at Carter and Co could have made Nicole Kidman feel like a frump, Catherine was sure of that. Sadly however, and much to Catherine's annoyance, none of the girls who had been so keen to have her come, had bothered to turn up themselves. For a while she'd feared she was sitting at the wrong venue, and decked out in the fashions she was, that could have been highly embarrassing.

Still, the murder mystery weekend was being held at a very sophisticated joint; some country house in the middle of the Cotswolds, with a full a la carte menu, free bar and room service. If Catherine was going to feel like a sad case, she may as well feel like one in the lap of luxury. It was all expenses paid, after all. Not forgetting that this contract was financially viable, with incentives and if it was to extend to a further six months, she wouldn't want to appear stand-offish by not joining in.

Everyone had glammed up in 1920's costume and, if she hadn't felt quite so self-conscious, Catherine might have actually realised that she was the most stunning female in the place.

'Ladies, gentleman and George,' the Managing Director's attempt at humour was met with the expected forced laughter of his minions.

'May I first thank you all for coming, and secondly for abiding by the suggested dress code, though I had expected the men to wear trousers, George.' Another deliberate pause for chuckles. 'Now Harriet has spent months arranging this, so not only do I expect you all to enjoy your change of surroundings this weekend, but also appreciate her hard work in organising death and motive. She has promised me some dramatic effects and surprise victims. Two victims and one murderer stand with us in this room right now, but all have been sworn to secrecy . . .'

'Or at the very least, bribed heavily,' interrupted a voice from the back.

'Okay, okay,' the MD struggled to regain everyone's attention, as sincere laughter now echoed around the walls. 'You will each receive a foolscap envelope with your names on and inside discover a little more about each other. Before any bright spark announces intentions to sue, may I take this opportunity to assure you that none of the facts are true. They are merely guidelines to help you adopt a new persona, but please do not share the contents of your pages, as they also disclose whether you are either killer, victim or suspect.'

The speech seemed endless as Catherine strained her neck towards the back of the room. The voice, the one who had cracked the joke about bribed employees, that voice had seemed suddenly so familiar. Yes, a little too familiar and not one from the office of Carter and Co.

As everyone collected their packets and new identities, their eyes met. Yes, it was James! No, he showed no surprise at all, just his usual cheeky grin. Far more composed than she felt. Catherine walked slowly passed him and whispered, 'If I weren't a lady, I'd throw this all over you.'

'Ooh, that would be wasteful,' he said, ensuring that no one could hear. 'You're always better off throwing red wine, white doesn't stain.'

Catherine slit open her envelope and slipped out of the room.

Her new identity was Eleanor Ross; a rich and very eligible socialite. 'Although she is not the murderer, suspicion may fall in her direction as she has had several, very public exchanges with both victims . . .' the sheet disclosed.

'I thought the closest you'd ever come to one of these gatherings was a portion of Death By Chocolate,' James was suddenly by her side again.

'Think a lot, do you?' Catherine clenched her teeth. 'Think about the feelings you crush and the hearts you break?'

'Now that's what I call holding a grudge,' he tutted dramatically.

'A grudge? You call what I must be thinking about you, 'a grudge'?'

'It was two years ago, Catts.'

'You jilted me at the altar.'

That finally shut him up.

As everyone else spilled out onto the landing, a large gong rang for dinner. James lifted his arm like an old-fashioned gentleman, and was immediately met by a young girl that Catherine vaguely recognised. She was the little redhead from the accounts department. Catherine had to look twice but, yes, there on her third finger sat a solitaire diamond. No one offered Catherine their arm, but she suddenly found herself accompanied by a rather large and grey-haired lady. 'Don't mind me, dear, apparently I'm Lady Ross' chaperone. I'm Daisy Pilcher.' Leaning in to avoid being overheard, she added, 'Actually, I'm Jean from the cleaning agency, and I don't know about you, but I'm not the murderer.'

As the party tucked into after dinner mints, Catherine took the opportunity of asking Jean about James.

'He's not from our place, is he?' she asked casually.

'No, love, but he is engaged to Penny from accounts. I maybe shouldn't say anything, but guests weren't supposed to be allowed, you know, staff only.'

'That's what I thought,' Catherine knew only too well, that once you could crank up a gossip, their tongues would run forever.

'You know Harriet, the PA who organised this whole charade? Well, there are rumours flying all over about her and Penny's beau there. Talk about the fiancee being the last to know.'

Catherine clenched her fists, then excused herself and retired for the night.

After a buffet style breakfast Daisy, well Jean the cleaner, caught up with Catherine. 'Were you not well last night, love? I'm supposed to be your chaperone, you can tell me if you're the murderer, you know. Nudge, nudge, wink, wink.'

'Sorry,' Catherine smiled. 'I was just tired, but . . .' With that a scream rang out from upstairs and everyone dutifully raced up to it.

There, with a fake knife sticking from a stream of ketchup across his abdomen, lay the managing director himself.

'I only went for a pee,' exclaimed a bespectacled young woman, obviously the voice behind the scream. 'When I came out of the bathroom . . .' she just pointed to explain the rest.

'What? You stabbed him?' laughed Daisy the chaperone.

'No,' frowns were visibly thrown in Jean's direction as she'd not remained true to her character.

Catherine took her chance and headed off up the stairs. Seeing James again had hurt more than she'd expected and all this talk of murder and woe fell far short of cheering her up. Even Jean the cleaner wasn't going to be able to do that. As she followed the grand staircase up to the next landing, she became aware of a figure. It was James.

'What are you up to?' She kicked herself for sounding too interested.

Tapping the side of his nose, he looked up towards the ceiling and then darted off down the corridor. Tempted to follow she may have been, but that hadn't been James' intention. If Catherine was correct, James was the killer on this weekend, and the rest of Carter and Co were welcome to him.

The next two hours were taken up reading Cosmo, and then a knock came on Catherine's door.

'Miss Ross?' A Hercule Poirot impersonator tipped his head in question. 'I am . . .'

'Yes, I know,' Catherine really couldn't be bothered anymore and held out her wrists. 'Take me, Inspector.'

'What?' A look of terror crossed the squat man's face.

'Take me, I did it.' Catherine could see Harriet fuming not five feet away.

'What is your problem?' Harriet snapped. 'Why would you try to hinder a murder investigation, like this?'

'I argued with both dead men, slipped the gaze of my chaperone and, the biggest crime of all, I actually brought a copy of Cosmopolitan with me.' Carter and Co's temp fell to her knees dramatically.

'Only one man's been murdered,' hissed Harriet. 'Don't betray the plot!'

'I sink zis woman should be seen by a doctor as soon as the body has been removed,' the fake detective stayed openly loyal to the script, even as Catherine slammed the door behind him. Then the penny dropped.

Staking out the upper landing for over an hour, Catherine's suspicions were confirmed.

'You're not the killer, are you? You're the second victim.' She came from the shadows as James arrived.

'Sssshhh,' he hissed with a grin. 'Harriet'll kill me.'

'Not half as literally as Penny will when she discovers you two have been writing your own additional chapter.'

'I think she already knows, my sweet. She's a bit like you that way. Buries her head in the sand.'

'What the hell is that supposed to mean?'

'You knew I wouldn't be at the church that day. You'd left more than enough messages on my answer machine, and more than enough texts on my phone. You knew I wouldn't be there, but you turned a blind eye. You play around with hearts and romance, love and marriage, and someone is inevitably going to get hurt.'

It took a few more moments for Catherine to compose herself, but eventually she spoke. 'You are the second victim here, aren't you?'

'Yes, well, Harriet can be very persuasive.'

'You make me sick.'

'So does red wine, but I've often seen you go back for more,' James began attaching himself to some kind of rope and hook mechanism.

'So you don't even see Penny as any more special than me, do you?'

'Girls? You're all the same.' Now James hauled himself up onto the banister rail.

'What are you doing exactly?'

'Feigning suicide. That should confuse the issue, eh?'

The idea had been that with one murder victim, then a suicide, people may wrongly suspect James, when in fact, his suicide was the second murder. Fine, if you love Agatha Christie, but tiresome if you're missing your pizza and Carte D'or.

Two bolts had been attached to the ceiling; one held a fake noose, the other supporting cable and wires. These latter workings would hold James' weight whilst the audience imagined the neck was doing this. All very gruesome, but completely applauded by Carter and Co's chairman, board and MD. Applauded too by Catherine, in a way. The plan was oh so simple, and James would never hurt another living soul. Glancing around quickly, Catherine knew that Harriet wouldn't be letting a soul near this landing. Nothing was to wreck any of her plans for this great murder mystery weekend. As far as everyone else was concerned, Catherine was taking a long, hot bath and had never been introduced to James and, let's be honest, this was all just a murder waiting to happen.

When the second scream went up that afternoon, it was clearly far more realistic than the first.

'How could it have happened?' sobbed Harriet. 'The bolt was held fast, the whole set up should have been able to support a small elephant.'

There, in the foyer of the hotel, lay the crumpled body of James. The mechanism had failed and he'd fallen three floors to a stone tiled floor. Luckily for him, smiled Catherine to herself, Harriet had come out to check that he'd committed suicide realistically enough. If anyone else had found him, he might have got a round of applause, so realistic was his corpse. Still, as the police said when they arrived, if people play around with ropes, heights, knives and murders, someone is inevitably going to get hurt.

SECRETS AND LIES
Anna Mills

She sat perched on a chair in her glittery black dress with her perfect curls falling elegantly onto her shoulders. A whole party bustled around her. Hidden in the corner she gracefully sipped her wine, scanning the room for a familiar face. Why has she really bothered coming anyway? A whole bunch of pretentious strangers, slapping each other on the back, congratulating each other on pure hearsay. It had seemed such an excellent idea to try something new, but now it seemed so incredibly wrong. Honestly, what had possessed her to attend a . . .

'Penny for them,' startled she looked to her side, framed by the back lighting, obscuring her view, stood a man. Remembering her manners she replied, 'Sorry, what did you say, and please, could you move nearer as I have only just started using contact lenses and you're a bit fuzzy.' Both of them burst into peals of laughter.

'I've been called many things, but never fuzzy,' he replied. 'I'm Jonathan Marshall and you are . . .'

Still feeling a little foolish, she ventured, 'Someone who would rather be anywhere else but here, 'Josephine, Jo Trantor.'

'Please to meet you Jo Trantor, looks like we already have something in common, I hate these stuffy, self congratulatory dos!'

While he had been talking she had given him the 'once over'. Mmm nice shoulders, she had always had a thing about men's shoulders, deep voice and slightly amusing way of speaking, thank you, thank you, thank you, just what she needed, some light entertainment.

Now was more in focus, she was able to see how good looking he really was, dark brown hair, slightly messy, she liked that, not classically handsome, with grey oriental shaped eyes, and eyelashes, to die for. Why was it that men always seemed to have longer, fuller lashes than herself? At this point she was conscious she had been staring at his mouth, mesmerised at how, when he paused, part of one of his front teeth was just visible, charming.

'Would you like a drink,' he proffered, 'I can see you've almost finished your wine,' and leaning closer, whispered, 'or would you rather get out of here? I know a late night jazz club where we'll be left alone.'

'That would be lovely, I don't know much about the night life, as I am here on business. The friend I was supposed to meet has stood me up.'

'You poor thing,' he added with a wink. With that he escorted her to the door, stopping only to retrieve her coat from the cloakroom reception, which he held for her. Stepping out into the chill of the evening air, he quickly placed her coat around her shoulders, pausing just long enough for her to feel a thrill run through her body as his hand brushed carelessly against her neck. Did he do that on purpose? The night is turning out better than she had hoped.

The Half Moon club was only a short ride away and the doorman nodded approvingly at them as they exited the taxi. Once inside, her senses were assailed by a heady mixture of music, chatter and warmth. Jonathan quickly took her coat, and spoke quietly to the maitre de, at which point they were ushered to a secluded booth at the edge of the stage. The booth was dimly lit with ornate candles, was that incense she could smell? Anyway, what did it matter, she was having a good time and the evening was getting better and better. She felt a warm glow spread slowly through her body, as she relaxed into the plush surroundings. She so deserved a treat, after enduring that ridiculous party.

She became vaguely aware that Jonathan was asking her a question. 'Jo, what can I get you to drink? I can recommend the champagne, or if you prefer, they do a splendid Shiraz.'

'Mmm, let me see, I would like some champagne, but I don't want to take advantage of your generosity,' she replied.

'Don't worry Jo you're not.'

Something in his voice made her sit up a little straighter, she couldn't be sure but he sounded a little strained. She must be more tired than she thought, the glow from the candle cast a somewhat waxy shadow across his face which disquieted her a little.

Next thing she knew, Jonathan snapped his fingers, and as if by magic, a waiter was pouring her a glass of chilled champagne. 'I must be getting old,' she said, 'where did that come from?'

Jonathan reached over and held her hand, there it was again, that thrill of excitement, skin on skin. 'Actually Jo, you nodded off for a while, I didn't want to wake you as you looked so beautiful. The black of your dress highlights the delicate paleness of your neck. You really do have the loveliest of necks, it was what attracted me to you in the first place.' His fingers held her hand tighter and raising her hand to his lips bit one of her fingers.

'Ouch,' she screamed, trying frantically to extricate her hand from his vice-like grip, 'that really hurt, what do you think you are playing at?'

'I'm not playing at anything Jo,' Jonathan replied fixing her with his stare and said, 'but I think you may be,' at which point she lapsed into unconsciousness.

She came to, with a sore head, the club was nowhere to be seen, instead she was in what looked like a wine cellar, and cold, terribly cold. She resisted the urge to scream knowing that to do so would be pointless. She couldn't be sure but she sensed that there were 'other things' in there with her. What these 'other things' could be made her feel crazy. Just then a wave of nausea overwhelmed her, crouching doubled up on the damp floor she searched for her handbag, but to no avail. Her thoughts racing she was afraid she would pass out again and pressed her fingernails into the palm of her hands in a desperate attempt to keep in touch with reality. The pain hit her like a thousand needles in her brain, jolting her senses. Shaking her head she determined to make sense of the night's events and how, dear God, how she was going to make it back to the hotel alive.

The sound of scratching caught her attention, looking into the gloom, she could see something moving. Too late they were upon her. Rats! For what seemed an eternity, she struggled to keep them off her, her revulsion at their squirming, hot, furry bodies mounting every second. Slowly she realised that instead of ripping her to shreds they were keeping her warm. She fought to regain her composure, incredibly she was actually gaining strength from their numbers.

The cellar door flew open, dust disturbed by the sudden movement of air was choking her with its acrid taste. What now, dear God, what now! At the point of collapse, the dust disappeared as quickly as it came, there, standing in front of her was Jonathan. At least it looked like Jonathan but he was hovering a few inches above the floor. Extending both arms he said proudly, 'I see you have met my, how do you say, family.' At the sound of his voice the rats moved as one to stand behind him, as mesmerised as she with the obedience his voice commanded.

'I-I-I . . .' her voice tailed off, desperately struggling to find the words, any words to express her fear. Exhausted she gave up, thankful that the wall prevented her from slipping to the floor as she stumbled backwards.

'There, there, Jo, I know this has been rather a shock to the system but do try and keep up,' he said mockingly. Her skin crawled with the cold and camp, she knew she was sweating as her once perfect dress clung to her tiny frame. She started to shiver, this has got to be some kind of nightmare. Before any more thought materialised, Jonathan took hold of her hand, this time there was no thrill of skin on skin, only fear, cold hard fear. 'You have a decision to make my dear. I'm not usually this sentimental, but, you have a certain indefinable quality, a luminescence I find particularly beguiling.'

'A choice?' was all she managed to say.

'Yes, a choice. As you have probably gathered, I am not what you thought I was. I am from a place you could not possibly imagine, even in your nightmare. I know, I have seen them. However, I am allowed, every few hundred years, to offer one of my victims,' here he paused to allow the full horror of the moment sink in, 'you are a victim Jo, three choices.' Jonathan paused, to Jo it seemed like an eternity. 'Aren't you going to ask me what they are? Cat got your tongue?'

'Stop it, stop it, your taunting is unbearable, tell me, tell me now, what they are!' The force of her voice shocked her. Even Jonathan looked mildly amused by her attempt to gain control.

'Firstly, you can be my victim, give up now, submit to my every desire. Is that shake of your head, a no? As much as I would like you to submit, I think I would be a little disappointed.' Jo, still reeling from being held captive, stared at him with utter contempt. 'Secondly, you can opt for the 'I'll give you a head start option', self explanatory really. I do like a good chase, one small point, I can fly and you, well, you can only run! Mmm, do I detect an air of resignation, Jo?'

'Just get on with it, I haven't heard the last choice!' yelled Jo, fighting hard to quell her rising panic.

'My, my we are impatient, aren't we, well here it is, the third, and in my opinion, the most attractive of the three choices. Join me.' With this he moved swiftly to her side, enveloped her in his arms, whispering, 'Join me Jo, join me. We would be so good together, I would be the envy of the underworld.'

Jo felt herself pulled into a vortex of uncertainty. She closed her eyes, all her fears melted away, she was floating on a magic carpet, high above the world, vivid images flashing in front of her eyes, she felt wanted, safe, happy, no more fear. Jonathan by her side, holding her hand, seduced by his touch she replied, 'Yes, yes, oh yes.'

They were back in the Half Moon, Jonathan frantically waving a napkin in front of her face. 'Thank God Jo, you were out for ages. I was getting terribly worried about you.'

'What happened?' was all she managed to say.

'You got up to go to the bathroom, tripped and fell. I'm so glad you are all right, you are all right aren't you?'

'Yes, I feel a little groggy, could I have a glass of water?' While she waited, she mused, it was all a dream, a product of a bump on her head, my imagination will be the death of me one day. Breathing deeply with contentment, she thought what more could a girl want, Jonathan is so attentive, so good looking, even with my fall, my luck is definitely on the up. Together they decided he would make sure she got back to the hotel in one piece.

As she stepped out into the cool night air, Jonathan enveloped her in his arms, the ground disappeared, replaced by a swirling cauldron of chaos. Before she had time to scream, she realised, all too late, she was starring in her own nightmare!

TRANSFORMATION
S Mullinger

She sat perched on a chair in her glittery black dress with her perfect curls falling elegantly onto her shoulders. A whole party bustled around her. Hidden in the corner she gracefully sipped her wine, scanning the room for a familiar face. Why has she really bothered coming anyway? A whole bunch of pretentious strangers, slapping each other on the back, congratulating each other on pure hearsay. It had seemed such an excellent idea to try something new, but now it seemed so incredibly wrong. Honestly, what had possessed her to attend . . . a New Year's Eve Ball . . .

Which was taking place at the home of her fabulously wealthy, often eccentrically behaved Godmother. Every year she was invited but a party in London had never appealed before. It filled her with dread. But this year's invitation had arrived in Annabel's Christmas card. Her Godmother was insistent that Annabel attend, saying she would not take no for an answer. It was this insistent tone which had created a nervous excitement in Annabel and which resulted in her attending her first formal ball.

But now she felt totally out of her depth although suitably attired for the occasion. Annabel had already had several moments of panic, had been telling herself she did not belong at this gathering. She did try to mix with the other guests, but wondered why she bothered because most of the guests were much older than her. They had no time for a mere chit of a girl. The few younger guests seemed to Annabel to completely ignore her. The only person she knew was Lucy, her Godmother, her hostess, who was kept busy mingling between various small groups of her friends. Annabel, stretched out her elegantly dressed arm and took another glass of wine, while she continued to watch nervously from the corner of the room. She fidgeted on her seat, trying not to bite her perfectly manicured nails.

Annabel was used to the large town house. She visited her Godmother at least three times a year. It was not the impressive surroundings which made her nervous but her own personality. The grandeur of the rooms were familiar, with enormous family portraits filling every available space. These did not daunt our heroine. However, after a visit, Annabel, was always glad to return to the rural outskirts of

Kent to her parents house, enjoying the quiet of the countryside where there was no need to worry about how she was dressed.

Catching a glimpse of herself in a mirror on the opposite wall, she hardly recognised the highly made up woman who was looking back at her. At home, she spent most days dressed in old stretched jumpers and comfortable jeans. Her hair was usually pulled back into a practical ponytail. Annabel suspected she was the only person in the room who felt uncomfortable by their own appearance this evening. She realised in London society people dressed up most of the time. But Annabel had not wanted to let Lucy down. Lucy had always been extremely kind to her. Annabel's Godmother had shown a keen interest in her upbringing. Lucy always remembered her birthday and at Christmas time purchased exquisite gifts for Annabel. When she was away Lucy sent postcards from her foreign travels. In fact, although middle-aged she acted more like an older sister to Annabel than her Godmother. Lucy had the ability to make Annabel laugh loud and long. A talent not many people possessed in the company of the nervous, sensitive girl.

Suddenly, her Godmother announced from the centre of the room that she had a speech to make. Perhaps everyone could follow her into the drawing room. It was a slightly smaller room and Lucy believed more friendly for what she now wanted to reveal. As the puzzled crowd surged forward, Annabel found herself walking beside a portly middle-aged gentleman. She had heard someone call him Mr Forsyth, recalled he was her Godmother's accountant. Even though, Annabel was still feeling nervous, she tried to make polite small talk, but decided that when humour was handed out Mr Forsyth, was definitely at the back of the queue. The gentleman completely ignored her remarks, in fact, seemed oblivious to her presence. Annabel noticed everybody else had paired off, thus, she trailed along at the back of the line. She headed for a quiet spot to stand and observe.

A large silver gong was struck, *how melodramatic! How passé!* Annabel thought, noticing all eyes were focused on her Godmother Lucy Caldwell. Lucy was a successful business woman, she owned her own company. This she had bought with money inherited from her grandparents. In the vicinity of her home Lucy was well-known for hosting marvellous parties. People were pleased to receive and delighted to accept invitations. New Year's Eve parties were always the best, less than a hundred people, an intimate occasion. Lucy, a spinster aged fifty, enjoyed a hectic social life. She believed all people are equal and treated friends, family and employees with the same healthy regard. After what seemed like an unending pause Lucy began speaking. 'Friends in a few minutes a new year will begin but it will end without me. You see I have some news which will shock and maybe even upset you, Annabel most of all. I have felt unwell lately, seen a doctor and had some tests. The prognosis isn't good, I have an incurable form of cancer.'

An audible groan reverberated around the room.

'Because of this unexpected verdict, I've had to do some really quick thinking. I made sure all my closest friends and work colleagues would be present tonight to introduce you all to my Goddaughter, Annabel. Come forward Annabel, come here, beside me. Now there are a few important work decisions I must stress to you all. First, I have decided I want Annabel to take over the running of the business as soon as possible. As you know I have no partner or offspring and Annabel is an orphan with no siblings. She has no ties, thus, I will arrange for her to move into this house at the earliest opportunity. Annabel listened, but could not take it all in. Second, I want you my dear friends to put aside any petty differences you may have, believe me I know about these, to help Annabel. She knows nothing about your business. Third, enjoy the rest of the party and that reminds me, quick everyone, raise your glasses to the new year, ten, nine, eight . . .'

As the countdown continued Annabel retreated back into the previous room, found once more her chair in the corner. Her mind was racing. Tears filled her eyes, her mascara started to run but Annabel did not notice. She felt stunned, afraid. How could she cope with the loss of her beloved Lucy, less than a year after the death of her dear parents in a car crash? Then it hit her, Lucy was leaving the company in her inexperienced hands. Lucy wanted her to live in London, leave all of her past behind. Annabel was shuddering, wished she had not come to this event. Lucy, she sobbed, she had forgotten how Lucy must be feeling. Oh! She was selfish, perhaps it was not too late for a cure to be found. Doctors were finding out more about illnesses every day. If Lucy remained strong there might be hope. Annabel held her head in her hands, no longer aware of her surroundings. Perhaps, she thought, this is only a bad dream.

But, she became conscious of music playing, through the open door, she could see people dancing, talking, laughing. Everything looked normal but how could it be? mused Annabel. No longer feeling like the nervous, excited lady of earlier evening, Annabel felt like a young child as her heart cried out for her parents, for Lucy, for anyone who would listen. Without a thought she marched into the drawing room and climbed upon the tiny raised platform. Annabel shouted into the crowd, 'How dare you carry on as if nothing is wrong, Lucy is dying, dying do you hear me?'

'Yes, we know,' fifty people replied in unison.

Lucy appeared at Annabel's side, she helped remove her to one side of the room and gave her a big hug. 'Darling Annabel,' she said, 'all the trials you are experiencing have to be for a reason. I know it's a lot I'm asking, but I want to know my company will be left in safe hands - your hands. You will run my company for me won't you?' Feeling scared, trapped, Annabel responded that she knew nothing about Lucy's business. 'But you will learn quickly, I can start teaching you and when I am too ill my friends will take over your education.' Annabel felt she was in the middle of a nightmare. The evening which had begun excitedly yet nervously for her, had ended with her petrified, could it get any worse?

The ball continued, laughter filled the rooms, as Lucy had planned, plenty of time to become maudlin in the days ahead. Lucy led Annabel upstairs to bed.

'Poor child,' one of the guests uttered as the women left the room. 'But, of course, we will have to help her. She looks very timid like a mouse caught in a trap. What an awful shock for her, for us, and especially Lucy.'

'Yes,' replied her friend, before taking another sip of her drink.

'Tomorrow,' said Lucy, 'I will start teaching you some of the basics of your new business. I will get some of the section leaders to come and meet you and they can explain exactly what work they perform. I do not want to talk about my illness - no I'm not being brave but am a coward. I need you to concentrate on work ethics because I have been told by a reliable source that my time left is short.'

Annabel interjected, 'You expect me to change my life, my home just like that a moment's notice. I do not understand why you did not tell me before about your illness. Why not tell me when we were on our own instead of in front of all those strangers? Watching them earlier, I saw a lot of back biting going on. It is obvious they all love you but not each other. How do I know which of them I can trust?'

'Darling, I knew this way would be hard but I thought you would find it difficult to turn down my offer in front of so many people. You won't refuse will you? Of course not! I only found out myself how ill I am last week. Decided to tell everyone in one go, hence my insistence that people attended this year's New Year's Eve Ball. Now get some sleep love, you have to learn the ropes of managing a fashion business - starting tomorrow.'

Annabel's life and fortunes were changed forever. The following day she began learning the baffling rules associated with the fashion industry. While Lucy's health deteriorated, Annabel's business acumen quickly developed. Transformation of character, changed Annabel from the nervous twenty-year-old, reluctantly attending her first formal ball into a shrewd business woman. The faith Lucy had had in Annabel was proved. A change witnessed by Lucy before her peaceful death.

Today, Annabel owns the largest fashion retailers based in London, with outlets based in every British city.

DOWN ON THE FARM
Clive Cornwall

She sat perched on a chair in her glittery black dress with her perfect curls falling elegantly onto her shoulders. A whole party bustled around her. Hidden in the corner she gracefully sipped her wine, scanning the room for a familiar face. Why has she really bothered coming anyway? A whole bunch of pretentious strangers, slapping each other on the back, congratulating each other on pure hearsay. It had seemed such an excellent idea to try something new, but now it seemed so incredibly wrong. Honestly, what had possessed her to attend . . . a reunion.

The first in fact of Unit X until recently classified Top Secret. The party was in fact in a village community centre at the far end of a large open green not far from 'the farm'. Unit X was the largest and deepest underground secret location with a history from the fifties to the eighties. Her mind wandered over her years there and how they used to arrive for work in the back of a lorry supposedly carrying cattle food or something agricultural. She had even arrived on a tractor and once on the top of a load of hay. Jane, known as 'Red' because of her hair colour, searched the room for a familiar face. And there was Ted Dexter, her old boss.

He was known as 'The Shepherd' and had been the third and youngest director of Unit X. The other two were long since dead. He now had slightly greying hair. And there was Fred Tillingham one-time deputy head. Close by the bar there were two black suited men with black specs looking like something out of a Bond film. No one seemed to know them, or at least no one approached them. Every so often they went missing, presumably to go outside for a smoke or some fresh air. Jane was feeling easier and tried to engage in conversation above the noise of the band who played mainly numbers from the decades that Unit X had been functional. From a tense start things were warming up. There, over there was sweet Jan, such a kindly girl and there in the other corner - no not that one - the far left was the all-time comic, Alex. It was not so bad after all.

The buffet was good and she had a dance or two. It would appear that Unit X really had been secure and all over the long years of operation there had never been any sort of security breach. The 'mock' farm ploy had worked.

By mid-evening the atmosphere was good and much mixing and talking and laughter was taking place. Ted Dexter called for a number of toasts including of course one for Unit X. Then he announced a surprise and requested that they all follow him. Torches were issued and the guests set off behind Ted. A path had been cut through the undergrowth which had closed in over the years since Unit X had ceased to operate. Somehow 'The Shepherd', with his influence and many contacts had managed to get light and power reinstated for the occasion. The party spent about half an hour at the unit. Memories flooded back. Jane almost longed for those times to return.

The party made its way back down the track to the hall. Most of the party were quite overcome. Such an unexpected experience. Jane noticed after a while that Ted was not in the hall, neither were the two Bond-like characters. Jane spoke to others about the fact that Ted was not there. The usual checks were made. No Ted. Perhaps he had gone to his car or back to the unit for some reason. Ted was found not far down the pathway. He was just alive. An ambulance was called and he was taken to the nearest hospital. Most likely it was a heart attack.

Fred Tillingham followed the ambulance in his own car. Others left for home. The celebrations were over. Jane stayed back a while to compose herself.

Alex came back into the hall looking drained and trembling all over. Jane and the others present went to his aid. Fred - Fred Tillingham - Fred was dead. Killed outright. His car had left the road only a half a mile or so down the road. It was a sad, sad close to the Unit X reunion.

Some months later Ted Dexter was still in a coma and hanging on to life. He had not had a heart attack and his illness was a complete mystery. The accident of Fred Tillingham was no accident. An investigation had shown that his brake pipes had been cut. Who had done this and why? Probably the two Bond-like men in black who just vanished. But no. They were Special Branch. But why were they there at all?

A year or so later Jane and Alex were married. They paid one more visit to Unit X on their special day to lay flowers in memory of friends gone, and the past.

OBSERVING THE FACTS OF LIFE
Mary Rice Ivor Birch

She sat perched on a chair in her glittery black dress with her perfect curls falling elegantly onto her shoulders. A whole party bustled around her. Hidden in the corner she gracefully sipped her wine, scanning the room for a familiar face. Why has she really bothered coming anyway? A whole bunch of pretentious strangers, slapping each other on the back, congratulating each other on pure hearsay. It had seemed such an excellent idea to try something new, but now it seemed so incredibly wrong. Honestly, what had possessed her to attend . . . a drab, uninteresting get together like this in the first place.

Casually glancing at the antique clock dangling like a gem from the wall high above the piano in front of her, she realised she could sit alone no longer. Hurriedly collecting together her girlie belongings she angrily stormed from the room. As she made her way aimlessly along the corridor, she failed to notice the precious oil paintings that richly enhanced the enchanting passageway. Bursting through the half open doors she now stood in a totally deserted street. As the refreshing breeze whispered softly through her velvet lapels her light coat swayed gently in the cool night air. She casually sauntered along the pathway heading back to where she belonged, yearning to be once more among considerate, down to earth, decent people.

As her parents' house could be seen clearly in the distance, she paused under the street lamp to look for her key. Reaching the front door she eagerly turned the key in the lock, 'Mum, it's me, Jenny,' she cried. As she entered the front room Lilly, her mother, with the front of her pretty printed cotton night-dress flung wide open revealing an awesome cleavage, sat awkwardly, holding her head in her hands, with her legs wide open in front of a blazing coal fire, allowing her oversized bosom to rest lazily on her knees. She shuffled lightly in an effort to bring relief to several irregular worm like mounds of varicose veins. Her prematurely ageing face displayed more wrinkles than a fine lined corduroy cap, truly dominated by a bulbous whiskey drinker's nose, which housed more pot marks than a pound of pickled pork. Gurning quite frequently she slowly rolled her pimply nicotine stained tongue over uneven salivated gums, revealing craters where decaying teeth were once displayed. The long hairs dangling from a conspicuously huge mole on her deeply dimpled double chin, danced despondently, desperately hanging on to their roots as she nagged relentlessly.

Fred, her father, stood by her side, with his round shoulders slumped in a slovenly manner, completely covered over with a home knitted, soup stained waistcoat. Obviously well past its sell-by-date, its ungracious hem hung loosely over his snuff encrusted trouser pockets, unintentionally giving way to nature's gravitational pull, on the well worn rosewood pipe that he had secured with a crude elastic band, to his badly battered tobacco tin. Disgustingly his beer drinker's belly hung in a heap over a dilapidated pre-war belt, that along with a pair of old khaki army braces held up his tattered moleskin trousers, yet Fred, content, filled with pride, though somewhat void of compassion, completely ignored Lilly, as he happily rambled on about horse racing.

Sister June, wearing the smile of a heavenly angel swaggered in, with her hair recently styled, looking almost as young as the day she was born, her soft, lightly tanned, unblemished skin glistened under a shadeless light bulb, speckled by facets of light refracting from her lip gloss, her dainty pearl earrings danced like pure magic as she seductively moved her gracious body around the room. Guaranteed to attract everyone's attention, this girl evidently content was sure of her ultimate potential.

Jenny's brother, Henry, leaned against a freshly painted kitchen wall revealing his hairy, masculine chest, openly displaying a heavy gold medallion which hung totally inert over the third button of his oriental style shirt, smiling broadly, he posed as if modelling for a mail order catalogue. Clearly unshaven his macho looks were being closely observed through the open curtains by a couple of bottle blonde slappers on the opposite side of the road, sitting quietly smoking a fix on their dingy doorstep.

Cousin Charlie, whose face bore the appearance of an apeman sucking a blind cobbler's thumb, sat piercing holes in fresh collected conkers, using Lilly's favourite hat pin for a bodkin. It looked as though someone had lit a fire in the middle of his face, deciding, as a kind gesture, to put it out with a shovel. He had truly unimaginable features, so bad in fact that no one could have thumped putty as ugly as he. The wires dangling around his fat, stunted, flabby neck, were attached to bright yellow plugs which protruded annoyingly from both ears. Nits, lice, among various other types of crawling creatures, adhered to the base of what appeared to be the tuft of a neglected mohican Indian haircut, where rather disgustingly, the near shaven sides revealed positive signs of a recent bed bug festival.

As he quivered, he jerked his head uncontrollably to the sound of whatever junk his under developed young brain attempted to interpret. The dew drop that teetered at the tip of his nose dropped to the floor, to be magically absorbed into the dirty moth eaten pile of the lounge carpet. In a flash, his saturated, slippery, silver coloured snivel laced shirt sleeve, drifted across his nose in an effort to ease the discomfort he now suffered, possibly due to the slow formation of another mucus based candle. The tattered, worn out trainers partly covering his feet gave off an odour similar to that of a decomposed polecat, dipped in camel dung, rolled up wet in an Arab's sandal, but he was happy.

Jenny's illegitimate daughter, Phoebe crawled around the kitchen floor, rolling around occasionally on an old fashioned felt rug making gurgling baby noises, oblivious to everything going on around her. Her dirty, flattened dummy caked in yesterday's strawberry jam lay on the mud stained tiles, hardly recognisable beneath a swarm of disease ridden flies. The smell from her bulging, discoloured nappy, almost made the pig, which they kept in the corner of the room as an air freshner, vomit, but no doubt someone would seriously consider changing it before the week came to an end.

Poluki the old German shepherd, sat licking his credentials, loudly snuffling as he snorted, content to make all sorts of other disgusting noises in the process. With one hind leg wrapped around the back of his neck, he constantly scratched as he fidgeted, impatiently seeking the location of an irritating flea, gradually shuffling along the rough concrete floor on his itchy bottom, thus indicating quite clearly, that the poor neglected mutt suffered from worms. The phlegm like matter oozing from poor Poluki's eyes, formed a thick secretion, which dripped onto the white-ish mangy patches on his back, though his nose seemed moderately dry. Quite naturally this unusually scruffy animal looked as if a good meal would not go amiss, yet in all honesty, he blended in well with this perfectly wonderful, riffy, family.

Higgins the cat lay across the draining board next to the untidy neglected kitchen sink, enjoying what was left of a bowl of soggy, mashed up, sweet smelling cornflakes. With one eye on Fred, the other stared continuously at the budgie cage. Occasionally he would stretch over like a contortionist, spreading his flea ridden carcass, enabling him to reach the conspicuous green spout of the dripping tap, where he quietly lapped up the water at his own leisure. The stinking sink teemed, full to the brim with dirty unwashed plates, sticky cutlery adhered to used crockery or to empty glasses, all noticeably marring this unfortunate animal's creature comforts. Still! even though he hadn't much room to manoeuvre, it looked like he knew how to live dangerously. Blind in one eye, with his left ear completely missing, battle scars adorned his lithe body like the ancient carvings on an American red Indian's totem pole, but he didn't seem to mind, for he purred well, knowing perhaps, that he had possibly one more life to his credit.

Joey the budgerigar, excitedly looked into his mirror, pausing now and again to tinkle his tiny bell, as feathers which had piled up amid rubbish over the past few months flew freely everywhere. His cage looked as though it had not been cleaned for the duration of his short neglected life. Debris, which should have been sparse, rested so thick underneath his perch, that he literally walked upon it. The unbelievable methane type smell from this poor bird's droppings nearly knocked Jenny over. Dangerous though it seemed the cage dangled precariously over the sadly neglected television, with its abhorred contents continually falling to form a huge mound of rank refuse above the TV screen. Yet somehow pretty little Joey thrived within the complexity of this dirty, smelly jungle.

No one spoke a word to Jenny, yet she did not care? For even though Jenny realised her family were not of the highest standing, she considered them all, decent, down-to-earth people, preferring their bickerings to sitting on her own surrounded by a house full of snobbish, stuck-up stuffed shirts. Tears welled in her eyes as she sighed, lovingly placing her borrowed dress, on the vacant hanger inside her sister's wardrobe, yet was it any wonder considering it had been her first real encounter with the outside world? For this modern day Cinderella, named Jenny the night had been a complete disaster.

INFORMATION

We hope you have enjoyed reading this book - and that you will continue to enjoy it in the coming years.

If you are interested in becoming a New Fiction author then drop us a line, or give us a call, and we'll send you a free information pack.

Alternatively if you would like to order further copies of this book or any of our other titles, then please give us a call or log onto our website at www.forwardpress.co.uk

New Fiction Information
Remus House
Coltsfoot Drive
Peterborough
PE2 9JX
(01733) 898101